I0547831

The Mushroom Effect

MICHAEL CONNOR

Ouen Press

Published in Great Britain in 2020
by Ouen Press

Suite One, Ingles Manor, Castle Hill Avenue
Folkestone, Kent, UK
www.ouenpress.com

ISBN: 978-1-9996121-3-9

A CIP catalogue record of this book is available
from the British Library.

Cover Design: Ouen Press, Main illustration:
istock/artisteer

To Max

OTHER WORKS
by the author

The Soho Don
May All Your Names Be Forgotten
The Cleansing

CONTENTS

AUTHOR'S NOTES

During Erminia's travels she reads a short story –
Under Fire – which has been printed in full towards
the back of the book.

PART ONE

Baby Magpies

CHAPTER ONE

Ground birds, the smallest first, followed by the pigeon-sized, break cover from dew-wet grass, sky-bound; moorhen and duck scatter for the sanctuary of the dark mud-swilled river. Both movement and sound have disturbed them from their camouflaged nests, but for this dawn it is not meat or poultry, nor fish, that are the purpose of the early morning forage. Over-head large birds, which may be geese, cruise on what appears to be a predetermined flight plan, unaware of the minor perturbation seven thousand feet below.

Erminia is of course not the cause of alarm, she is thirty to forty metres back having travelled lightly, but now stopped and off the toe-path on the opposite side from the watercourse. She calls quickly, knowing Bianco will plunge in after the flapping of wings and squawking dissonance without a second thought, if not reined-in by a stiff command.

It is the middle of May and the sun is breaking the horizon. Civil twilight is about forty minutes earlier at this time of the year. Erminia will drive in the dark to a favoured or new destination with potential. But she prefers, as she did this morning, to be placing her steaming coffee in the dashboard holder and shutting the door of the passenger seat behind Bianco as the deep black of night is being sanded thin.

For the selection of greens and herbs Erminia needs, she spends a number of hours locating, picking and packing her wild food into her various poacher's bags. Gentleness at the point of the pick, she believes is essential to preserving the delicate flavour during transport. Some of her harvest may be used for garnish, so the leaves need to be whole and uncracked, while those that may end up pulverised by mortar and pestle, must be able to relinquish all of their juices for the mouth. Treated without respect, broken leaves will release sap, which attracts flies, dust and other airborne pollution. The less leaves are washed, the greater the retention of the magic she is depending upon.

She has sat for a while over breakfast – rashers of dry cured British Lop pig, fried in a pan above a small fire, and sandwiched between slices of sourdough baked in the kitchen yesterday and now toasted over open flames using a forked stick cut for the purpose. It is minutes off midday, the pickings have been thinner than normal, she wonders if others had been scrogging what she now, after many months, has come to consider her personal patch.

Bianco satisfies his voracious appetite gained from being outrun by a dray of grey squirrels and rabbits by the colony. Brought up on a diet of raw meat, not derived from his hunting prowess, but chicken chopped and prepared by his owner means the chasing provides ample sport, as opposed to nutritional destitution.

Erminia wipes the pan using a handful of long bladed grass, in the knowledge the sucs will feed the unseen life of insects, and then she does the same with the licked-clean dog bowl.

A distant church bell chimes noon as the two drive the Defender out from under the trees onto the narrow, once-blue, metal road.

Normally Erminia would return home to sleep for a couple of hours and then around three-thirty head into work to begin the evening mise en plus, as the restaurant is only open for dinner. But today this will not be possible. A meeting with her accountant and the manager of the business section of the local bank has been scheduled for a review; Erminia judges this unnecessary and believes the event has been arranged to allow both to submit their bills for 'additional' work. Crowdfunding had resulted in them both losing out on substantial fees they could have expected to earn for arranging loans. Both seem to have long memories.

The drive back goes almost directly passed the turn-off into town, where her meeting will be and the following turn-off leads to the restaurant. But Erminia takes neither, despite the fact a clean blouse and trouser-suit hangs on the back of her office door, and the shower facilities back of house are good. That would have been the easiest thing to do, but she drives on out another four miles so Bianco will not have to spend the afternoon and evening confined to the

Defender. It had been one of the facilities cost forced her to abandon when she had searched for the right location to open '*De Regio*'. The lack of an outside area had been a disappointment; an elegant Italian style terrazza for her customers and a run for Bianco. But customers did not miss what had never been, and Erminia was prepared to drive the extra miles for Bianco's well-being.

Angela works from home, it is her cottage and Erminia moved in when the lease on her own place had come up for renewal. At first Bianco had been a distraction, the puppyness was still in him very strong then and Angela regularly complained at having a dog around when she was trying to work.

'It is not conducive to either concentration or creativity. A crazy Italian woman is one thing, but a wild Italian animal…'

Now her hand constantly drops to her side unconsciously looking to stroke the wire Spinone coat of the strong gentle giant, even when his bundle of flaxen fur has gone romping off down the garden to return mud and foliage bestrewn. Today she will not be there.

A large beef bone, a weekly treat courtesy of the butcher will keep Bianco occupied, and a tin bath filled to the brim with water from the outside tap will ensure he has sufficient to drink until Angela's homecoming, or if delayed until Erminia returns, but that is generally not much before midnight. Earlier and the till will have suffered.

o0o

Swapped into the relative comfort of the Jag, Erminia swings into the car park outside the restaurant every inch the chef/patron, transferring the poacher's bags into the cold room before walking the half-mile across town to the bank. The early morning sun has clouded over and a dismal feel purveys. Had the parking not recently become a matter of luck in the town, she would have taken the car. The idea of getting soaked on the way back does not appeal.

At *De Regio* ninety minutes later, soaked, stripped and changed into her whites, Erminia seeks to bring her mind to enter its creative mode to start the preparation for the evening menu. The brigade will clock-on later; this is her *zen* taste-time. Peaceful, no distractions, a flavour capsule when she will finalise how the dishes on the table d'hôte must be finished and presented. She is the host and it is her table and it is these dishes, her dishes that have brought in the business, brought in diners from outside the county, sometimes outside the country. This afternoon however the host needs to kick herself. The meeting at the bank had not been the rubber stamp she had anticipated.

Erminia sets out a sample from each of her bags in the order she has picked them, checks them against the notes transposed to her iPad – the listicle showing both common and Latin names, plus picking record:

The Claytonia – Montia perfoliata
– picked close to parking spot.

This she decides will form part of a garnish for the veal dish she will be offering.

The Stinging nettles – Urtica dioica
– picked close to the tree line.

These young leaves will be the dominant flavour in a broth to be served with a salsa verde sauce originating from the Lombardy region and spread on rustic chunks of toasted focaccia.

The Dandelions – Taraxacum officinale
– picked in the open area of the grassed paddock.
  The buds slightly open.

It is decided these will form the second part of the veal garnish.

The Sorrel – Rumex acetosa
– picked in the paddock close to the dandelion.

This she will turn into a pesto and serve with turbot caught today and to be delivered by the fishmonger after closing his shop at the other end of town.

Normally she would have been more adventurous, maybe, but the choices made today are far from mediocre.

Whereas Monday is her day off – everyone's day off. *De Regio* is closed, there is no other host, she does not trust her reputation to even her most talented. In February, there is no service at all. She and Angela had skied, Bianco got lost in the snow. Jaysie, her talented sous, had ventured to the Caribbean. Some complained that August was when they wanted to take their annual leave, but Erminia was firm, it was part of the contract. Being employed – chosen – to work at *De Regio* , to work under Erminia was an honour. It was a price to be paid. Families were constrained to simmer on the back burner. Or, if you wanted to go to the top, into the chill cabinet.

So, Monday is when she takes her mind off food and focuses on all the other things that were essential to running a successful restaurant. The things that were required to operate any successful business. But it would be five days before the next Monday showed it's face! It was like saying 'don't think of polar bears for fifteen minutes'. Polar bears were not even in the far distant Siberia of your mind two seconds ago, now they won't go away – the glaciers of your consciousness are covered with them.

Erminia takes a doorman's large sixteen ribbed, sixty-two inch umbrella from it's holder. The clouds are still threatening but the downpour is for the moment at least finished. For a full five minutes she stands on the opposite pavement staring at the front of her establishment. Her accountant prepared the financial statements for the florist adjoining as well, in fact it was the owner of this business that had recommended him when Erminia was canvassing the local shopkeepers before signing the lease on her property.

The last thing she had wanted was to be landed with a next-door neighbour selling everything for fifty pence, or almost as bad, one of numerous charity shops that had become more prolific than Starbucks and McDonalds combined. Was there really so much secondhand furniture and such demand for relics of the tasteless dead? But no, this end of the town seemed to be surviving well and the view of the other shop owners was that the opening of a fine-dining restaurant could only help the area thrive.

Things had now changed, not that the assumption had been wrong, quite the reverse. The florists had gone from strength to strength, so much so that the property they inhabited was no longer capable of fulfilling the need.

According to her accountant, their accountant, the greater part of the trade was represented by weddings, funerals and corporate events. The decision was taken to ditch the shop, and the ever increasing cost of rent and rates, and work from larger more suitable premises on a nearby industrial estate, maintaining a presence on the main street by taking a window and corner of a tea-rooms a dozen or so doors up.

The florist was on the point of putting her name to an assignment of lease in favour of a global fast food franchise, when the accountant asked if she would wait until he had spoken to Erminia.

In the early days, Erminia been a regular visitor to the shop, like a bee to honey, but when the owner's daughter, Clare, took a job in New York, the visits became fewer. Business at De Regio became more demanding before long, and when Angela who had been brought in to help with the interiors remained on the menu, the excursions into the pollen filled jungle of sweet scented exotic blooms and erotic stems had not ended, but had become genial rather than lustful.

It's possible, there were certain financial attractions as well as the obvious aesthetic implications – no groups outside throwing their stunted-growth cycles recklessly across the pavement, wheels spinning; no groups of discarded wrappers, cartons and canisters adding to the obstacles; no groups waiting for their sweetly spiced greasy fuel to be called while they puffed smoke of various aromas into the path of arriving guests. Over the last eighteen months the town had become more vibrant; planning for a dozen five bedroom double-garage houses on little more than a postage stamp had been given consent, and an insurance company with it's headquarters in Japan had taken over a block that had been vacant almost since its completion. The accountant had run some figures – wine, cocktails, craft bottle beers and light lunches as a subsidiary using the existing De Regio kitchen facilities was financially compelling.

From the window opposite Clare's mother is beckoning her over.

'The people that have the unit I want are demanding I sign the lease in the next few days. We've known each other a while Erminia, I'm prepared to give you first chance but I've got the assignment on my desk. If you want it you'll have to move fast,' she tells her.

If she doesn't take it, Erminia knows she could soon find guests reluctant to expose themselves to rubbing shoulders with people who spit in the street. A restaurant in decline can soon face a self-fulfilling prophecy. She has never experienced it personally but she had read about it in the trade press and worked alongside chefs who had found themselves very quickly out of a job.

oOo

'Erminia, I think that is one of the finest dishes I've tasted. You are a genius with flavours.' The man making the compliment is not a critic, but with his nationwide network and booming voice reverberating wherever he went, she considers his praise and patronage to be as important if not more so than any of the food pundits.

Patron Erminia is unable to steal accolades from another; her appreciation of the culinary art and her own integrity will not permit it.

'I have to admit that particular creation was Jaysie's, my sous chef. One day she will run her own kitchen and have Michelin stars raining down on her. And I'll be a proud person to say she worked in my kitchen.'

Today is the first occasion Erminia has handed over responsibility to anyone for the creation of a dish served on her menu. Time had just evaporated. The business of the business had eclipsed the magic of the chef's table.

Is it a decision she can make overnight? The service may be possible, but there is also the set up cost to be considered. True, the accountant had satisfied the bank manager that the increased business could service the debt with sufficient conviction the loan would be offered. Going out to crowdfund a second time would she believes gain little additional support, and the timing to develop a campaign will not fuse.

The weather is not cold and as she pulls onto the gravel at twelve-twenty, she hears Bianco come into the garden ready to nuzzle against her thigh as she pushes open the gate under the spot detecting both their movement. Angela is dozing on the sofa having killed the engine of the van on the drive a little after six, eaten, fed the dog and curled up waiting for Erminia to return.

With Bianco on guard, asleep on the scullery floor, Angela and Erminia climb into bed without any sort of conversation. Angela has driven a hundred miles there and a hundred miles back with a set-up of her garden sculptures in between. It has been a long day for her and her partner knows that even with the assistance of the curator manoeuvring, placing and reconciling the final positions with those shown in the programme, it was both tiring and tiresome.

On normal days where possible Angela had regulated her working pattern to match Erminia's. She would rise early, as she heard the two ramblers driving off and head down to fire up the small forge in the outbuilding at the bottom of the garden. Most of her work was metal based, in winter she would work inside soaking up the heat from the glowing coals; in the warmer weather the hard standing outside allowed her to hammer and twist the anatomy of her art and soak up the essential essence that she found most invigorating. It was their thing, making love in the shower: Erminia would return, cold and muddy or sweaty and dusty and she would join her in every way possible under the scalding heat of the shower torrent in colder months or under the ice cold spray in summer. Either would only rinse the grime away. Their own satisfied cravings would perform the core cleansing. Angela and Erminia would sleep for a couple of hours and when the chef left for the restaurant, the sculptor would return to the forge and mangle contorted human shapes many people found difficult to diagnose, only returning to the cottage shortly before her lover was expected at the onset of night.

In bed now, Angela kisses her and is gone almost before their lips part. Erminia stays, stays awake, conscious and when she does doze her subconscious joins the quandary. When she gets out of bed the following morning she is more tired than when she laid down, five hours earlier. Had it not been for Bianco scratching the bedroom door, she would have rolled over to chase her slumber once more. As she pulls on her clothes she looks at the covers, Angela, still dead to the world looking like a figurine set in royal icing on a top-tier. Her own side has taken on the appearance of a plate of part-eaten mille-feuille.

She needs to put it to bed, she tells herself, and quick.

Yesterday she had neglected the very foundation on which her culinary success has been built. Allowed another person to exercise control of a critical part. So, it had proved to be of the required standard, but that need not have been the outcome. This morning, now, she wants to sleep. In the back of her mind she is calculating the extent of the stock in the cold room and if it's condition allows it to be usable. Bianco saves the day.

They drive eleven miles, it is the closest foraging patch of the fifteen on her listicle – next to each location the past and potential harvest is described. Some of the plants are shown as not expected to be yet fully in leaf or in bloom this week of this month. But the weather has been unseasonably warm, so it is her hope enough will be ready. The site is earmarked for a visit early the next week in any case.

There is no running water at this location. A substantial walk along a narrow footpath, bordered on each side by crop cultivation, leading to an area where hedgerows meet and a small copse, provides for wild ground cover leaf. Bianco keeps predominantly to the well walked lines, gone for handfuls of minutes out of sight on deployment for some unknown, unseen quarry, before returning panting and collapsing close-by. Rarely blood blotches his muzzle, successful kills are rare.

Erminia is reluctant to take the meagre amount. So far from abundant, and in scavenging the lot she worries about threatening what could be precious bounty as spring turns to summer. She should have driven further, patches where she knows there are proven crops of early growth.

Again her focus is on more not better. The increase generated by the cocktail bar thing set against the perfection of her current passion - De Regio .

Back at the cottage, delicacies placed in the chill of the commercial refrigerator in a corner of Angela's outhouse, they soap each other's skin, slip slide in the wet heat with nimble fingers, searching tongues and shower toys. And now they sleep. When they wake, Erminia wants to discuss the predicament in which she finds herself and the restaurant. But if the decision proves to be ill-conceived she does not want it to be a responsibility she seeks to share or step away from. Any mistake must be her own. It reminds her of her best friend at school taking the blame for something she had done, which was so insignificant she can no longer recall the deed. But her friend's punishment had been to spend a full school day locked in the stationery cupboard. Erminia had vowed never to allow anyone again to take onus for her transgressions.

In her car, Erminia phones the Bank and makes an appointment with the business manager. After various transfers and struggles and a mid-lane swerve, its settled for late afternoon of the next day. Then she sends a text to Clare's mother telling her she will be in contact on Monday with the intention of moving forward. Subject to the success of the meeting, she hopes this will allow her to take back control of her mind for the weekend service.

o0o

Each table it transpires is booked, two sixes wanting to be away early both heading, although it appears not together, to a gala presentation at the Guild Hall. Second sittings on these tables would allow for the takings to be higher than projected, although invariably the kitchen will close on the late side.

'One veal, one eel, one lamb.' Erminia stands at the pass waiting for the reply to come back like an echo. And it does.

'Yes Chef.' The three chefs tasked with these dishes cry in chorus.

It is a table of six, but unlike most aboyers, Erminia does not call all the dishes at the same time. She calls the order in view of the time each dish takes to create on the plate. A dish taking ten minutes will be called ten minutes after a dish chef determines will take twenty minutes to be brought to the pass. In most kitchens, this calculation will be left to the individual chefs to compute, but Erminia is a control freak to the nth degree. Is this a fault? Well she knows that if it is, it is one that allows her to sleep at night.

The pass is quiet, generally; the occasional repositioning of a petal tooled with long fingered tweezers, the soaking up of a still melted butter splash nearly not visible to the naked eye with the corner of a tissue, the critical view by the specialist pupil looking to pursue fault. Rarely did the atmosphere become explosive, but on occasions it did and in these isolated events the person responsible on the other side of the hotplate would inevitably vacate the arena to be permanently replaced by an understudy chomping at the bit to don the whites of the De Regio . Tonight all is as Erminia would hope. Is this due to the decision she thinks she has come to?

The paperwork from the bank arrives by email as promised, shortly after ten on Monday morning, with the request to sign and return the hard copy the same day if possible. Erminia reads the loan agreement line by line. Any thought of not telling Angela until after the deed was done is now manifestly impossible. At the last meeting, the business manager had indicated the loan would be subject to a legal charge on the various properties. In the small print this clearly includes the cottage. Did they not realise the family residence was not hers, not even partially hers? She calls the bank. Regardless, it appears the loan cannot proceed without a charge on a freehold property – commercial leases did not provide the requisite security apparently. The no-risk status for the lender despite the fact business was about, as Erminia had been told on many instances, risk and reward; surely the lending of money is a business she muses.

Angela takes Mondays off to coincide with Erminia. She does not want them to become ships in the night. Erminia does not forage on a Monday, but so Bianco does not miss out on his daily exercise and the weather being pleasant, Erminia would regularly order a picnic basket from a wonderful deli in Lechmead, and spend the afternoon relaxed in some breathtaking locus. Three of her favourite foraging spots have been found on these excursions, although at each time she has logged it secretly in her thoughts and returned alone to evaluate closely the original sense of the place.

On this Monday she books a table for dinner at one of Angela's favourite restaurants along the coast. And then cancels it. The thought of an intense discussion burgeoning under the observation of staff who would report any tempus between them to industry insiders, and in front of customers she knew were also many of her own regular guests, did not appeal.

Angela was angry.

Very few things made Angela's blood reach the proverbial 100 degrees but one of those things had just been discharged down the phone into her ear. The displeasure divulged by the curator of her most recent exhibition forces a spate of phrases from her mouth that turns the air blue.

'I hate that man,' she declares. 'I'm never letting him near any of my pieces ever again.'

Reticent to proceed with her own news and the implication surrounding it Erminia toys with the distraction of a chilled Villa Bucci, Riserva, a Verdicchio imported from a personal friend living a few kilometres outside Ancona. Having pulled the cork, Erminia has poured the wine into a glass allowing oxygenation. From her limited vantage point stretched out across the tartan picnic blanket, Angela is asked to close her eyes during the tasting to test her palate and determine if the wine being tasted is red or white. It will not be exposed by temperature as the

better the vintage the closer to ambient temperature
the finer the nose of apple, honey, hazelnuts and herbs
in a yellow straw liquid.

Erminia's friend believes the greatness of this wine
is in some way due to the fact that Bucci, the vineyard
owner also grows durum wheat, peas, sugar beets,
olives and sunflowers, a man who understands the
earth as well as the wine.

'Of course it must happen darling. It is a wonderful
development. We will do whatever is necessary. Phone
the bank and the florist now. No, right now. Have you
thought of a theme, I think an atmosphere that slowly
shrinks away from De Regio, do you imagine
connecting doors?'

Today Erminia has chosen to serve the wine with,
and she does believe it to be this way round, potted
shrimps made in the deli using brown shrimp, clarified
sheep's milk butter, mace, cayenne and bay leaf, lemon
juice, sea salt and ground white pepper. And, from
completely the other side of the world, California,
who's wine she avoids, a Humboldt Fog goat's cheese
that she adores, eaten with Stillroom grilled melba
toast.

Angela is always ravenous after they make love and
they always do – which she attributes to the wide open
spaces, the sheer nature of everything. Still naked,
Erminia will open the second bottle and they will
continue to feed each other on veal tartare, quails eggs
which Angela attempts to shell using only her toes, and
pickled vegetable for their acidity.

Back at the Defender while packing up they will eat
chocolate in five personalities, each conjuring up sweet
thoughts of what tomorrow might bring.

oOo

No more than seven weeks pass and Angela is standing in the middle of the stripped-out florist's pondering the thought that she now boasts the ownership of Clare's beau and her shop, well her mother's shop. Had she been jealous? She questions her motives on a glance out of the window. A summer storm scatters pedestrians into doorways, seeking shelter from the exaggerated gauge of the drops. If she had been, it was not something of which she had been previously aware. The thought amuses more than troubles her. She drops the postcard sized scuffed black and white photo of Clare she has recovered from between shelf planks in a fitted cupboard onto a pile of other detritus swept into a corner, awaiting the arrival of a skip, and continues busying herself with visualizing the interior details.

The micro leaf and flowers used at De Regio arrived regularly by special delivery from specialist horticulturists, so the loss of the florist will not impede. Today the couriered packaged contains three buzz buttons and the deepest purple of orchid buds.

Erminia is concerned that the signing of the lease will pull her even further away from her culinary art and not allow her return until the florists – *il bar* as it is to be dubbed – has been transformed. But this proves not to be. Angela has no commissions on her slate and with the exhibition works finished and on display she is without clamour to produce. She is both content to sit back to assess the critical success of the show and to get her brain teeth stuck into the transformation of the barren shop into a stylish proposition.

Angela is now taking Sundays off to synchronise with the trades she is directing; the project being spread over thirteen weeks. This allows the work to be completed without an increased cost of overtime, a luxury the bank balance is happy to avoid and there is little point in being all dressed up with nowhere to go as regardless of the Chief Constable and the Head of Planning being regular guests at De Regio, the duration the courts and the Council take to grant the necessary licences and change of use seems intransigent.

The couple have become what they have always sought to avoid, vessels passing in the dark. The after lunch shower and the passion that went with it is now a pleasure of the past. Once il bar is up and running, everything will get back to normal Angela assures when Erminia carps .

'It is all for your benefit don't forget,' she adds, letting her know she should be grateful.

As the opening date grows closer, Erminia has still not made up her mind concerning the staffing arrangements for the lunchtime offering. Jaysie seems the obvious choice. She has been showing signs of interest, popping in and out more than intermittently as the design begins to take on a persona of its own. A twin, but not an identical twin.

Jaysie is talented, il bar needs a chef with flare – the question in Erminia's heart is *Could dinner at De Regio flourish without her?*

Finally Erminia decides to float the idea with the notion that the position and the monetary offer she has modelled will be both expected and embraced.

'Fuck you Chef.'

Jaysie stamps her foot.

'Just fuck you,' she repeats the scream, now an emotional crackle breaking into the pitch.

'Jaysie, it's a good offer. I don't know why you're so mad.'

'This place should be mine. I thought that was the whole point. So you could step aside without losing face.'

'Losing face... losing face what d'ya mean losing face?' Erminia's tone is filled with incredulity.

'I'm a better cook than you'll ever be. You heard what whatever his name said, best he's ever tasted. That was mine. Me. We could have two Michelin stars if it was me.' It pours out now and is followed by a stream of Italian parolacce.

'You're not even Italian, wallyo bitch.' Erminia rebuffs, knowing Jaysie hates the second generation taunt.

'Cornuto' Jaysie spits.

And before Erminia can speak, Jaysie turns and rips off her apron and hat, discarding them as she flees.

'It's you that needs to find a new home, Jaysie. You're finished here.' Erminia's words clash with the slamming of the back door.

Why she is bringing Angela into the slanging match Erminia is unable to fathom, '*wallyo bitch*' she mutters repeating the phrase to herself.

o0o

Angela is still up sitting on the sofa, sketching, when Erminia gets back to the cottage. Erminia starts to relay the astonishing outburst Jaysie has displayed.

'I heard,' Angela confides . 'It's why I stayed up. Would you like me to talk to her?' She adds.

Erminia thought Angela had left before all this nonsense erupted, but she has obviously been mistaken. She looks at Angela slightly confused.

'She might take it from me and you won't lose face. Now's not the time to be running with one of your top assets on the lam.'

'You think I want her back in my kitchen?' Erminia raises her voice as she feels her stress level returning.

'Stop being such a stud. You need her. We need her.' Angela says filling her tone with a reassuring warmth.

'We?' Erminia does not heed the verbal stroke.

'I've got my house on the line in this little adventure darling, so yes… WE.' Angela's voice has turned from purr to more than slightly clawing.

Had the purr come from a cat, Erminia would have flicked it with her foot in the direction of Bianco for him to tear into. Instead she runs a foam bath, a signal they use with each other to indicate they want some time alone. Time to soak and reflect. Later in bed she encourages Angela to take the top, dominate their love making and signal her submission to the unpalatable.

o0o

Bert, a great poissonnier of long standing at De Regio, proves unable to bring about the dominance to succeed Jaysie. He stays as sous on the following service with little noticeable improvement, and then on the third day Jaysie returns. Nothing is said. Nothing by anyone. The brigade return to their routine as if nothing has happened. But of course it has.

As the honeycomb tile floor of il bar begins to provide the facelift to the once rustic florists, and the pastel shade walls with forest greenery wallpaper in accent setbacks nears finishing, the staffing of the facility begins to overshadow everything.

Erminia does not say in any musings with Angela that the two senior positions for il bar worry her; that she is doomed to fall into a default situation of working a straight fourteen hour shift. Lunch at il bar and dinner at De Regio .

'Dark furniture has been de rigueur for the past I don't know how many years darling.' Angela announces when they view the catalogue of contract furnishings together.

Bohemian is the word that best describes the style Angela finally persuades Erminia to go for.

'This is 2017 for God's sake!' she taunts.

Friday, 1st October is the date set for a soft opening. No publicity, no ribbon cutting, no embossed invitations. The plywood screens that the Planners have permitted to encroach onto the pavement, removed Thursday evening and the doors open at 11 a.m. the following morning. Ease the staff and the systems in gently.

Erminia had met Tom on a couple of occasions at Hotelympia, the Salon Culinaire demonstrations, and his name had also started to appear in the trade and colour section of the weekend presses as someone to watch. Mid-twenties, photogenic, a rising star and a breeder – a trait she feels will be a positive balance at management level with Jaysie playing up. She makes the call and signs the employment contract in the last week of August. It costs her more than the Jaysie package, but Tom is bringing a name and that came with a price tag. The cocktail barman she steals from a trendy nightclub in Margate that had opened in a penny arcade with fanfares, but had proven lacklustre.

During the summer, the number of covers at De Regio remained high, with tourists filling the seats as regular clientele vacated in favour of their annual decamp to the exotic fleshpots of mainly the Med. Despite the coolness between the chef and her sous, service performs at a level commensurate with the time when il bar was still trading as Bloom-in-Dales – Clare's mother had been brought up close to Ingleborough Hall, home of Reginald Farrer, the famous Edwardian botanist and plant collector.

Erminia is first horrified and then elated. By midday on the 1st, the 'soft' aspect of the opening of the new venture is anything but. But Tom and the Margate émigré can't be faulted. The PR company that had handled the launch of De Regio achieves the same success with il bar – *delightful food, wonderful ambiance not encroached upon by overly slick service* and much to Angela's gratification, the interior is noted as being *avant garde*. The media carries no adverse comments.

CHAPTER TWO

The location is not new to Erminia. She has been
harvesting leaf here for some two and a half years.
Bianco knows all the smells and scents from boundary
to boundary. But with her poacher's bags more than
sufficiently full, and close to the edge of a somewhat
marshy pond, only now taking on water adequate to
justify its existence after the heavy deluge experienced
over the past four days, Erminia spies 'Baby Magpies'.
Or, what she believes to be 'Baby Magpies'. Had she
and Bianco not already enjoyed their breakfasts,
cleared up and doused the fire, she would have been
more than tempted to sauté a few off. Not a good idea
on reflection naturally, the flavour of the bacon would
mask some of the flavour of the Magpie if that's what
it is, and she isn't even sure of the toxicity of the
species. In the back of her mind, her memory rests on
the word edible. She picks three, gently places them in
a plastic sandwich bag she carries specifically for this
eventuality so there would be no opportunity of

contamination of the picked leaf. Then, using her smartphone she takes a picture of the small parliament. She is conflicted, mushrooms – fungus by any other name is tricky stuff.

'Are you crazy Ermi. You could have fallen unconscious eating something like that and suffered a contorted death before anyone found you.' Angela declares, truly aghast at the thought, as Erminia relays the characteristics of her dawn discovery.

'You must leave a note with where you can be found in case anything bad should ever happen,' Angela says thoughtfully, then adds, 'but I guess you can be traced through your phone.' Now sounding somewhat relieved.

'Location on my phone is turned off and besides I don't want to be tracked. Each of these places are secret to me. Much of De Regio's reputation is founded in these places. Anyway most haven't got a signal so…' Erminia's voice trails off, she does not seek to disguise the note of defiance in her tone and fails to fathom why after so long Angela believes her safety has suddenly become an issue.

On her laptop in the office Erminia googles what she is reasonably confident her find has been. Certainly she has no record, and her cataloging is pedantic, of the *Coprinus picaceus*, more commonly the Magpie Fungus at any of *her* sites.The list of edible fungi is legion only surpassed by those considered poisonous. But she is sure.

Using scissors, Erminia gently cuts open the sandwich bag and carefully tweezes the three specimens onto a plate. She expects the caps to have begun deteriorating by now, turning from the compact flesh of the everyday White-cap supermarket mushroom to a more slimy substance, foul smelling. But she is not even sure this characteristic applied to the Magpie, it may she thinks only relate to the Inkcap. Another peculiarity that intrigues is the impression the 'Baby Magpies' appear fully formed, despite the fact they measure only 5cm along the stem and slightly less than 3cm in diameter.

Without discussing her intention with Angela or any members of the brigade, Erminia decides to take the bull by the horns, to eat a small amount raw and a similar amount cooked. However, on reflection this does not seem sensible until after service on Sunday night. If the worst happens and she becomes violently ill, she will have the whole of Monday and the early part of Tuesday to stage a recovery. The thought of being laid up when the restaurant and bar are operational is not to bear thinking about. She has never taken time away while service is being offered. In the interim, she places the fungi in a small plastic container and seals it with a couple of turns of packing tape. DO NOT USE she inscribes in red felt tip before pushing it to the back of the top shelf in the cold room.

Research had indicated, and it is something she thinks she already knew, that some fungi are only poisonous in their raw state. This causes her over the coming days to ponder how best the tasting should be managed. She knew of none and had not heard of any fungi that transformed from non-poisonous to poisonous after the cooking process. On this basis she opts to eat the raw piece on Sunday night, and if no ill effects are encountered, prepare the cooked version on

Monday morning. If of course the first eating proves pernicious, the second experiment will have to wait until a later date.

oOo

Sunday evening all the tables are booked, but unusually all the guests ask to be seated early and even with a couple lingering over coffee, the room is empty and the doors locked shortly before ten-thirty.

Erminia's original plan had been to eat the raw fungus at work, but on the spur of the moment she changes her mind, drops the plastic container into her bag and guns the engine back to the cottage.

Any thought Erminia entertained that she might slip ignored into the kitchen, quickly evaporates. Angela is unexpectedly hovering in the hallway, a tall glass of champagne in each hand. Erminia diverts through to the living room. Even before Angela speaks her physical glee signals a celebration is required. Her dark eyes glitter, cheeks flush in recognition this is not her first glass.

'Guess what?'

'I don't know. Tell me.' Erminia answers, trying to muster enough enthusiasm not to dampen Angela's apparent euphoria.

'Guess. At least try… For me.' Angela giggles.

'It's our anniversary and I've forgotten and you're not mad.' Erminia says, knowing this not to be the case. And had it been their anniversary she knew Angela would be as mad as hell. 'Angie, sorry I'm tired, it was a busy shift.' She continues, lying a bit but she is just a little tired along with being more than slightly stressed at the ramifications of what might follow her tasting. If she can escape to make it happen that is.

'Three figures. Three fucking figures Ermi. Three fucking figures.'

'What on earth are you talking about,' Erminia asks now completely lost as to the topic of Angela's tirade.

'Some Russian oligarch, some South American drugs baron, an Israeli arms dealer, I don't know but someone, who cares, one of the guests invited to the showing has come back to the curator offering a three figure budget for me to furnish his garden. Can you believe that? Three fucking figures,' Angela blurts.

'Angela that's great, but can you please stop saying that.'

'The curator gave him my number and he's calling early next week to arrange for me to view and sign contracts.'

'That's wonderful. Truly, I'm so pleased for you.'

'For us Ermi, for us. Glamorous celebrity chef and stylish sculptor hand in hand. Do you think we should get married,' Angela enthuses, finishes her glass and refills it.

Erminia finds the thought a tad mind boggling. It is not something they have ever discussed. It had never been an issue. *Was it an issue now?* she silently asks herself, and avoids the answer.

'So where is this man of wealth and taste whisking you away to?'

'No idea,' Angela replies thoughtfully. It had obviously not been a question that as of yet has been of consideration.

'It could be the other side of the world,' Erminia speculates.

'You could come with me,' Angela offers after a quiet moment of reflection.

'And what about the restaurant?' Erminia speaks sharply, more sharply than she intends.

'It won't be forever darling and of course I know you can't just pick up sticks. That's your baby like this may be mine.' Angela recovers realising she has said something stupid and needs to show consideration.

'It'll probably turn out he's just bought Leeds Castle or somewhere just down the road. Let me just pop this lot in the kitchen and get changed and then we can finish the champagne,' Erminia suggests backing off and unslinging her bag.

With the precision of a Damascus steel blade, Erminia shaves a fine slice from the cap of a single Magpie, and another from the stem; at some point over the last few days this has been something she has further decided upon – to eat a sample from each part of the fungus, from the cap and from the stem and from the skirt – an edging located to the bottom of the stem she believes to be notoriously the most likely container of any poison.

Twenty minutes later Erminia's deed is done and they have adjourned to bed with the bottle. Angela does not normally sleep naked. She likes blacks and reds, rarely mixed, one or the other and strappy stuff. She would often not unpin her long black hair, but tonight it falls in a length almost sufficient to mask her tear shaped breasts. Neither Erminia nor Angela sought to be top on every session, taking, in unspoken turns, the dominant demands of their sexual desires. "The Happy Andros" a friend had called them. Again unspoken tonight, but not passing without a curious musing by Erminia that Angela in her elated state relaxes into that of a subordinate participant.

Erminia's own orientation at this moment appears unusual to her. Everything she sees seems over-defined and her eyes she knows linger on every detail longer than she imagines is normal for her. Angela's skin, the tall penis-erect shape flutes, the bulbous C-cup shape of the door handle, all become objects of intense scrutiny. Legs, which Erminia kneels between, are unlike most women she has sexed, they meet at the top of her thighs and her shoulders are distinctly wider than her hips.

Erminia's mouth is dry, her tongue feels rasped.

'Posso avere ancora un po' di vino?' Erminia whispers.

Angela in response gently drizzles a stream of Bollinger from the flute over her Brazil trim of her ripe and honey wet fig – a term they both use in homage to Ken Russell's Women in Love, rather than the close verbalisation of the Italian slang expression.

It is 4 a.m. before they fall asleep. The last thing Erminia remembers is wondering if the enhanced sensations she felt were due to the slivers of Magpie or something inferential between them.

No alarm has been set so it is close to eleven when Angela rouses, pulls herself out of bed and makes a mug of instant coffee which she sips sitting, still unclothed, in a corner of the garden, the rays of the late autumn sun conveying warmth. Bianco deprived of his breakfast bounds down the lawn in search of sustenance and alternates between irritating and cute in an attempt to goad Angela into action. Had it not been for this diversion she would have masturbated. She wants to, but finally concedes to the greater impetus, finds Bianco's empty food bowl and heads for the kitchen.

Erminia slept late on Mondays, although this usually amounted to getting up around ten and returning to bed with a cup of coffee, then working her way down a list of business calls before showering and planning the days indulgence. Thank God no-one ever suggested Facetime, she would smile, cradling each D cup and feeling for lumps during ring tones.

This morning, this Monday morning Erminia is dead to the world. Angela, with Bianco out of her hair and otherwise engaged, showers and dresses before taking a cup of French-pressed coffee through to the bedroom.

Erminia eventually stirs at the back end of twelve believing at some point during the night her limbs have been wrenched in unnatural directions. Maybe they had. She smiled at Angela who is perched on the rib edge of the bed, takes her hand and kisses the end of her finger tips.

On the other hand it may not be due to their intensive love making but the result of her pre-bed snack. Erminia now ponders whether she should try a taster of the cooked version. In the shower, her nipples and vagina are painful to touch but she feels that is par for the course. Her joints are painful, yes but virtually all the research on fungus poisoning entailed the early onset of vomiting and diarrhoea plus in most instances severe abdominal pain. She is experiencing none of these.

The decision now is could she cook the *Coprinus picaceus* without Angela noticing or with the thought that the most dangerous part of the experiment has passed, involve her.

She opts for openness. She will prepare and cook the slivers and if questioned, will not be deceitful.

In preparation for this mornings tasting and in the light of her decision of openness Erminia removes the container from its place tucked out of sight at the back of the fridge, takes the second one, one of those ones that remain whole and slices it lengthways in half. Still firm, not slimy, a slight smell which may have been present from the beginning but she would have expected something slightly more unpleasant, what really intrigues her is the power of the blood red, which if she chose to be generous could be purple. The colouring appears to be restricted to the inner crown of the cap, the gills at the height of the stem area. The fungus guides she has read all strongly urged the avoidance of red mushrooms as these are considered by most to always be toxic or psychoactive. *Amanita muscaria*, commonly known as the Fly agaric or Fly amanita being the reddest. The first of the three now comes under the same scrutiny and on cutting gives up an even deeper red. The third, a very similar shade.

Erminia's eyes are inquisitive, seeing but not believing, not understanding what it is she sees. The previous evening she had, without too much attention or ceremony shaved off a fine slice of the cap and similar from the foot of the stem, she had been in a hurry, not wishing to be caught and having to explain, argue and no doubt end up fighting over her intention to try the Magpie. Had she seen what she is now examining Erminia wonders if she would have been so brave.

Erminia does not see Angela standing in the doorway. She remains invisible until at last she speaks. It is only when Erminia places a nob of Normandy Beurre de Baratte into the skillet that Angela voices her opinion.

'Ermi what on earth are you doing?' The question does not really require an answer, she knows exactly what her partner is about to do. Her tone is firm, not angry or panicky, but sufficient to stop Erminia in her tracks.

Angela is not pacified, even after being told this is to be the second tasting and that on the previous it had been eaten raw. Finally she leaves the room with the stated intention that she is not going out for the rest of the day if Erminia goes ahead with her ridiculousness because she doesn't intend being embarrassed out in the street when an ambulance has to be summoned.

By the time Erminia has turned her attention back to what she has been doing, the pan contains a coating of beurre noir. Had she tasted the mushroom cooked previously and survived unscathed, sautéing in black butter with a squeeze of lemon might have been a choice. But for this experiment, the more natural flavour she considers preferable.

Bianco contents himself with racing up and down the garden, jumping four feet off the ground at low flying seagulls seeking snacks locally to avoid the twenty mile trip to the nearest landfill. Angela sits quietly at the window sketching something in her head and Erminia explores online any comments she can find relating to the red tinge she has found in the *Coprinus picaceus*, while she waits for her body to be struck down. By six-thirty it has not been and neither has she been able to locate any reference to the gills or any other part of this mushroom displaying the characteristics she's found.

She reads through the description found in most explanations of the growth:

- Substantially larger, height of 25 cm width of 5 cm.
- The cap being an elongated finger shape with a cone type opening. It appears white and dishevelled with a black background turning brown to grey to black and then slimey.
- The gills being white turning pink to grey then brown until becoming black and slimey.

'Not red' she says to herself out loud.

- The stem being white, slim and with a white skirt, often stained black from the spores and a lightly hairy bulbous base.

- The flesh itself maintaining white, while the spores being black.

- The odour emanating from this fungus is repellant.

Also by six-thirty, with the sun going down Angela vacates her position at the window and that of non-participation. She kisses Erminia on the neck and tells her she is pleased that she was still alive. They laugh. They order a take-way and with Bianco they curl up on the sofa and watch the Wachowskis's Sense8 on Netflix.

CHAPTER THREE

Nutty, no question about it, distinctive throughout the cap and the stem, although only when cooked. Uncooked, it is difficult to determine any flavour at all. The part that intrigues Erminia the most is the red area which again, when raw, offers very little. But when cooked, sautéed or lightly poached, her tastebuds, although struggling, whisper crayfish. Erminia is confused. The red, therefore the crayfish flavour, should not exist, but there is the rest of it; the fact that the "Babies" are fully formed and the flesh remains solid. After the second tasting, she has experienced no heightened awareness or any other reaction. Of course, it is too soon to contemplate introducing even the smallest amount into a dish to be included on the menu – the reason she picked them in the first place. And anyway, scientific research resulted in the poisonous status - DO NOT EAT, based on the cognisance that adverse consequences were experienced by *most* people.

Erminia knows if she is to have any hope of exploiting her find she needs to carry out 'clinical trials'. The question is how best to go about it. Seek volunteers or be less overt.

She decides to seek Angela's opinion.

Today is Sunday and now out foraging for leaf at the site Erminia currently refers to in her head as the Magpie place, she notices a distinct change in the weather. It is dry, but the temperature has markedly dropped. The dishes on the menu will need to start reflecting the wintery chill of more regular northerly winds.

While breakfast, a pan of two salsiccia, sizzles away softly, Erminia wanders to determine if further parliaments of Magpie are growing beyond her original patch – which she saw when first arriving is still flourishing. Bianco bounces at her side knowing his own plate of food is imminent. On the other side of the pond, but further from the perimeter there are signs of small mushrooms having protruded through the ground but currently only broken stems remain. It appears these Magpies, or potentially another small fungus of another species, have been trodden down. There are no determining footprints. It could easily have been walkers straying from the beaten track, badgers scurrying across or Bianco's hefty eighty four pounds doing the damage.

The sausages, hot with chilli flakes and strong with aniseed from the freshly grated fennel, are one of Erminia's favourites. This batch is slightly hotter than some. Each mixture she compares with those her mother makes and smiles at the perfection of the family recipe. She wipes the sucs with the remains of the focaccia, torn and warmed on the stones forming the low wall around the burning sticks. In her notes Erminia logs the locus status with special attention to the possibility of a second 'Baby Magpie' crop. Before leaving she picks eight of the 'Baby Magpies' in preparation for the tasting she has planned for the next day.

Sunday evening dinner is dead.

She sent the waiters and commis chefs off early, less from a sensitivity towards the staff and more to detract from the depressing aura that emanates from excess bodies hanging around. Erminia knows it is amazing the strangest things customers pick up on.

She calls Jaysie up to the pass and retreats into her tardis of an office, leaving the door open so she can maintain sight and sound of the little action taking place. Now looking to create three recipes on paper, two hot and one cold, all simple, no complex flavours to mask the delicate possibilities presented by the red 'Magpie' gills. She has come to the conclusion that the mushroom experiment will be more palatable if offered up within the constituent parts of a dish in favour of merely spooning the flesh onto a plate.

oOo

'It looks like the top of your fig Ermi' Angela muses. 'I'm looking forward to eating that one.'

For the last of the three dishes, Erminia has confit the small dark red area of the gills in a deep melt of Normandy Beurre de Baratte. The Damascus blade finely opens the flesh to form a butterfly appearance.

'It makes me shudder just watching you do that,' Angela says displaying a physical flutter of her upper body.

Erminia is preparing two small plates of each dish so they can try them together, each experiencing the whole. But has indicated the substitution of the 'Baby Magpie' at this stage for a supermarket variety to initially test the general concept of the overall dish presentation. A lie she feels confident will not cause any dire consequence but will avoid any great protestation.

'What do you think?' Erminia asks as they finish the first mouthful of a ravioli with a gentle herb seasoned mascarpone.

'I'm not sure.' Angela comments while contemplating the reaction of her palette.

The second plate is cold, a shaved salad of baby artichoke, celeriac, wild garlic leaves and dill fern drizzled with an olive oil and champagne dressing. This contains the largest amount of the deep red gills in the knowledge the raw pungency is least noticeable.

Angela champions the raviolo of the two, but is holding out for the final prospect.

Zucchini flower, imported, deep fried in a light tempura batter to provide a crunchy texture to the dish but then split open to expose the bloom, the confit butterfly perched and splashed with a beurre blanc nectar sits astride.

In each case Erminia has realised if the crayfish tinge is to be of any value it must be able to withstand the presence of at least subtle accompanying enrichments and although the red gills of the *Coprinus picaceus* are the largest if not in size but quantity of the ingredients, individually they do not outweigh the integration of the remainder.

Angela is so predictable Erminia concludes, as she, like the butterfly lands on the zucchini option. Erminia is not surprised as this is also her preferred plate. Both in taste and presentation. With Angela's choice and confirmation of the hint of crayfish, although she actually calls it crawfish, in the bag, Erminia now waits to monitor the onset of any adverse side effects.

There is nothing either good or bad, but thinking makes it so.'

How or why the voice of Hamlet comes into Erminia mind at this moment she is not sure, or even if Shakespeare's quote is relative to her seesaw attitude on the personal ethics of her deception.

Erminia has no worries of ambulances being called to the High Street or some autumn picnic spot, accessibility only along an unmade muddy track. Today Poland is sending winds in gale force loaded with sufficient water to drown fish. Bianco is refusing to leave the house and is emulating a fur rug in front of the Aga, with the ambition of moving to the sitting room to continue his fur rug disguise in front of the logs when his charges settle.

Erminia would have watched *Bound* for the twentieth time, but Angela fights for *Jupiter Ascending* and wins. They eat from bowls watching the Discovery Channel. They kick the dog out to do his business. They make love, they sleep.

o0o

Angela has had no knowledge of her guinea pig status and after discussion with her prospective client and much persuasion from Erminia, she agrees to travel to Paris – the designated meeting place – by train on the following Monday. This is not so Erminia can accompany Angela, but to allow her a whole free day to visit each of her hole-and-corner locations on an expedition in search of and to ascertain possible qualities of her newly discovered ingredient.

Come Monday, Erminia hugs Angela, wishes her luck and as dawn threatens is driving out, with food to cook and soup to warm, and the intention of visiting the most distant locus first and working her way back. As far as Angela is concerned she has left for her usual foraging trip to gather greens for a broth she regularly prepares at De Regio but will make at home for a supper in case Angela is hungry on her return. Erminia has not confided in Angela.

Oh Wonder's *All We Do* fills the cab, and Erminia is in a state of euphoric anticipation, despite having been stuck behind a farm truck for miles. She has taken note of the band and how they came together, changed and made it. But the thing that has stuck, other than liking their music is the way they promoted themselves. Is there something here she could learn she wonders. Releasing one new song every month for a year. Baby Magpies, one new dish each month, not a selection of half a dozen all at once, make the guests wait, anticipation, drip feed and then at the end of a year a Baby Magpie box on the menu, a tasting box.

Erminia arrives two hours or more later at her first field of plenty. Although it isn't. Bianco pee's everywhere possible and chases things that appear not to exist while his charge combs every square inch, turns every leaf, rolls every log and stone without success. The day goes on and the sites fall one by one with no evidence of even the *Coprinus picaceus* being present, let alone the 'Baby Magpie'. Forty-five minutes before the darkness in the sky matches the misery in her heart she arrives at the last location empty handed. The same note scrawled against all previous stops – None.

Bianco's energy is not suffering the same setback and before Erminia can bring him to heel, he receives a severe scolding and is dragged back to the confines of the Defender for trampling the larger of the two patches that must now be relied upon. This is more than a misdemeanor. She gathers what she can and is considering the creation of some kind of fence around each of the two parliaments, but does not for fear of alerting any unwanted *buttinskies* to the true wealth of the place.

Angela arrives back on the chime of midnight, wined and dined beyond legal limits, a contract in her courier case, her mood jubilant punctuated with bouts of dejection. The reason she will explain once she has reread the schedules and exhibits attached to the documents foisted upon her. But that won't be tonight.

During Tuesday afternoon, after an early morning forage that yields sufficient in greenery but adds little extra in the way of 'Baby Magpies', Erminia begins creating small dishes incorporating various parts of the mushrooms which, as members of the brigade arrive, she requests they eat and comment. Only later does she realise this could be suicidal for De Regio – potentially a grave error. The bookings for the evening are not substantial, but if each of the chefs were to experience adverse effects it could close the kitchen. The culinary telegraph, much like the clatter of a falling tray of spoons, will sound out the epidemic of food poisoning to foodies, trade and clients far and wide. Erminia is tempted to call her PR company to be on standby to prepare a crisis communications plan. Her mind is racing. But with further consideration she decides to wait until or if chefs start disappearing in the direction of the bog and echoes to her barks are not forthcoming.

As service begins, she stands at the pass scrutinising each member of her team, an ashen face, a facial grimace, a hand grabbing at a stomach – that pre-knowing twinge. No signs emerge, checks come in, food goes out, everyone performs their part without interruption.

Erminia is all smiles. She wonders if this is not premature, will they all turn into puking sweating trembling aspic heaps once arriving back at home. She has observed them for five hours, surely she thinks in that time there would have been some reaction. The next test will be to prepare canapés to pass round in il bar – on the house. Her confidence she knows is mushrooming and at the thought she quietly chuckles at the unintended pun. Back at the cottage she is remiss in not questioning Angela about her concerns over the contract and knows this, but is intolerant of invasions into her own world. The pace of her ambition is strengthening. Although the quantity of her find is minimal, she interprets this with a positive spin.

'I tested it out on the staff tonight,' Erminia offers up lightly as if she believes it is of no consequence.

'What did they think?'

Erminia shrugs. In truth she doesn't care. She knows the worth of the find, her only concern is the fact she might have the potential to poison large numbers of people and destroy her business.

By Friday, the busiest lunch at il bar, Erminia has replenished her stock, prepared the amuse-bouche trays for circulation, and takes a chair at a corner table to sip a Virgin Mary. If it was not a work day, she would have instructed the barman to thin the blood aggressively with a double quantity of Absolut.

Most customers stay less than ninety-minutes, it would have been just under the hour mid-week. She watches each mark pass through the door, and out onto the street. A few are detouring via the loo but none appear to be in the throes of some deathly hell-bite.

Erminia knows she must wait for the results of this test but she is pleased the guinea pigs number 101 when she does the totting up. If it affected one in a hundred, would that be such a price to pay? She can turn the whole thing on its head she imagines. One percent of the customers might suffer consequences, but to dine on this unique delicacy surely the gourmet cognoscente would demand to be allowed to take the risk.

Think fugu she tells herself. Maybe it will be worthwhile the PR crowd marketing De Regio in

Japan. She is conceiving an ad with a 'Baby Magpie' being used to bait a pufferfish.

CHAPTER FOUR

'It could be a new species darling. You might have discovered a new species. How wonderful.' Angela is honestly astonished. She grabs Erminia and hugs her. 'Magpie Erminia Fungus. You'd have the right to name it. That's what it would be known as.'

Dwarf Magpie Fungus is what Erminia has envisaged. But Angela is right. Why not.

'Are you sure Ermi, you'd look a absolute culo if you're wrong,' Angela says using the Italian word for arse and stepping back, looking Erminia in the eyes.

'I've googled it, researched everywhere possible I can find. I popped into the library and looked through old encyclopaedias. It's a dwarf I've found, but the flavours are compounded and as far as I can tell it doesn't contain the toxin of the large species.' Erminia is speaking with authority, the words tumbling out. 'It's part of the *Psathyrelloideae* group, I think. It's native to the UK. Found first by the French mycologist Jean Baptiste François Pierre Bulliard. That's the proper

size one I'm talking about. I found the dwarf one…
Magpie Erminia Fungus.' Erminia repeats proudly, the
'I' she lifts in tone.

Once again Erminia's focus is being
outmanoeuvred, this time not by the business of the
business but by the implications that surround the
discovery of MEF – she has decided to use only the
initials to ensure a level of security. Her worry is that if
the growing season proves to be the same as the larger
species it will finish at the end of November. Whilst
this she accepts from the stance of a locally grown
ingredient, she is concerned about the verification of
the fungus. Time is advancing and knowing the snail-
like pace of large institutions, she is circumspect that
registration of her discovery can happen with such
speed – if registration is how the process works; she
has no concept.

Her thought is to set up a small cultivation facility.
She has had this thought before, to grow other short-
season wild greens herself – but she is a purist. 'Wild
Food', is the expression used on her menus and in all
the PR company produced publicity. But what if, come
August there are no signs of the MEF pushing through
the soil? What if the MEF never again materialises?
She would be seen as stupido, a laughing stock.

Fugu is farmed. Scientists believe the highly
poisonous trail running through the pufferfish, that
part, which if inadvertently leaked onto the raw edible
flesh is sufficient to kill thirty human beings, is derived
from items digested in the food chain. So fish farms
have been established where all possible toxins have
been excluded. Has fish from this source been

downgraded, perceived as inferior? No risk, no honourable euphoria.

A further thought crosses her mind. Maybe a licence will need to be introduced and only those achieving the highest standards will be permitted to serve MEF. This could be something she could promote on par with the Japanese legislation. In the first instance of course MEF will only be available at De Regio. Maybe I will control the licences, the product only sold to those purveyors I'm prepared to supply, she mulls.

At the cottage, Erminia constantly discusses her discovery and Angela is spirited in her contribution. Little is said about Angela's three figure fee, the project or the contract, but Erminia fancies there is activity there not being thrashed out at home.

A plan formulates with surprising speed and with only the smallest of disagreements. But at the juncture of introducing the PR company to the scenario, Erminia again backs off from consenting to their involvement, completely unwilling to share her discovery, good or terrible, with outsiders.

With only the shortest notice, Angela flies out to the States at the request of the three-figure client to meet the landscape architect and interior design team. On her return, three days extended over and above the four working days originally scheduled, Erminia has created a new strategy. She will use the wild spores to cultivate sufficient MEF to maintain an ongoing supply throughout the winter, facilitated by appropriating a small area of Angela's workshop to benefit from the near constant warmth. She will work on creating one recipe capable of grandstanding the uniqueness of her discovery, using the PR company contacts to gain a place on the popular Professional Grande Saucier Contest, which is televised and broadcast to viewing cohorts of up to six million each time.

'Clare recommended me,' Angela confides while Erminia chops Zebrune banana shallots, which she is attracted to not only by flavour and lingering taste but also the tinge of pink to compliment the blood red of the MEF gills.

Sex in the shower and the spooned sleep siesta has been sacrificed for the development of the dish towards its final presentation.

'Clare who?' Erminia asks, paying only the slightest attention.

'Clare Blooming Dale' Angela replies, supplementing her surname with that of the shop, as she watches the cook's knife blade working in rapid chop-chop speed without a blink.

A lack of comprehension as to how Clare, the florist's daughter from next door, could have recommended Angela flashes through the extremity of Erminia's consciousness but she does not bother to pose the question.

'Can you pass me that?' she asks, pointing in the direction of a Parisienne spoon.

Angela obliges.

Each recipe is devised in Erminia's head, created in the late morning in the cottage kitchen, tested and refined in the late afternoon with the brigade who have been summoned to arrive earlier than normal.

Erminia has declared her intention to stand as a contestant in the next season of Grande Saucier, but has failed to entrust her chefs with the details of her discovery. It is a risk, she acknowledges to herself. But, while each chef has unquestionable prowess and mastery in their chosen niche, she harbours doubts that any of them hold sufficient expert knowledge in world of fungi.

They all eat the samples, but no probing questions are proffered. Any curiosity surrounding procurement and food miles, Erminia brushes aside with obfuscations and explanations of overriding exigency. To win will be kudos for De Regio and every member of staff employed. There is palpable excitement each time a dish is declared finished – a perfect example of the ingredient combination.

Erminia challenges herself to continue to ignore Jaysie's capability, talent, the great gift she possesses. 6-4, 6-4, 6-7, 6-7, 9-7 a tennis match, volley after volley, backwards and forwards, improve, improve again. Jaysie always pushes it back, better each time, adding more, taking away, the tennis match is Wimbledon Final 2008: Nadal vs Federer. In Erminia's head it nags she might not be Nadal, but the De Regio is hers – she finds the talent, she employs the talent, the talent is hers.

Ten dishes selected, every dish original, each considered by the brigade as perfection. On the following Monday all will be in the kitchen, all have agreed to give up their day off. Every recipe will be cooked again, and by majority vote the finest three will be selected.

With the ten now at three, Erminia has invited Tom, the Margate émigré (who is continued to be dubbed this due to him also being a 'Tom' – in the bar he tells everyone he is called ME, using the initials of his tag), Angela and Jaysie to the final tasting that will identify *the* dish Erminia will submit with her entry to the Grande Saucier contest.

The ingredients do not form part of the submission, only a short description of finished offering. Erminia simply uses the generic word *champignon*.

oOo

Each dish is permitted a twenty minute preparation time and a further twenty minute cooking and finishing time – forty minutes in total. This, Erminia believes exceeds the time for dishes one and two, while dish three with no complications should be achievable. Chairs have been brought into the kitchen, chilled wine, still mineral water and a selection of palate cleansers; chilled parsley and cucumber soup, mint sorbet and a celery mousse are on hand. Erminia has already spent the time allotted on each dish prior to cooking – so her guests, her recipes assessors, her *judges*, will only wait twenty minutes between each plate presentation. One and two are primi dishes and dish number three, a secondi.

The whole process takes almost two hours, as the guests wish to discuss each dish after it has been presented and naturally, also following its consumption. Erminia is not inclined to cook whilst these post-mortems are being conducted.

'So which one do you think I should cook?' Erminia poses the question to all, but seeks each to give their individual comment. When the last one has offered their opinion there will be a winning dish, although Erminia does not feel obliged to be trammelled by the result.

There is not one dish that receives a bad review, all are given high praise. Each guest has their own preference, but appreciates Erminia must be the one who makes the final decision. It will be her on whom the cameras will be focused. It will be her under scrutiny .

The second dish, Erminia declares as her favourite and is supported by a small round of applause.

'No,' Jaysie says too loud for her dissent to remain under her breath. 'No, it must be the third one, it's crazy to even consider the other two. The third one is more complex, it shows a greater skill, everything about it should be better.'

Angela, sitting to Jaysie's left, puts her hand on the sous chef's arm in a pacifying gesture.

'I could. I could,' Jaysie blurts out as she pushes Angela's hand away. 'You know I could Ermi,' she adds, unusually using Erminia's friends' abbreviation, instead of 'Chef', at the same moment flicking her heel to shove her seat away, then bursts into tears as she clips her hip on the edge of the stove that briefly hinders her accelerated pace in the direction of the door.

With the cooking all done, the tasting finished and the silence following Jaysie's embarrassing outburst over, Tom takes the chairs back to the restaurant as the rest of the staff wish Erminia well and leave.

'I'll be in the car,' Angela says

'I won't be long, I'll just check everything's locked up and I'll be there,' Erminia assures her.

Outside Angela is talking to Jaysie who she has found sitting hunched up on the car park wall, holding her hip and angrily kicking her heels against the brick. When Erminia comes out, she heads directly towards the Jag, avoiding engaging in the chinwag. Angela calls her over, but Erminia shakes her head, declining, clearly not wishing to become involved further in a Jaysie tantrum and creating a public spectacle. Reluctantly, Jaysie allows herself to be encouraged from her perch and with Angela's palm firmly in the small of her back they arrive at the car to the purr of the engine. Erminia has no intention of winding the window down, but coaxed by the heat of Angela's stare presses her finger momentarily on the button to power the glass down a few inches and that is the extent of her compromise.

'Jaysie wants to say sorry. She was out of order,' Angela says turning her glare on the mumpish Jaysie while at the same time applying pressure to her back. 'Jaysie apologies,' she prompts as no words seem to be breaking the ice.

'I was wrong to sound off the way I did,' Jaysie begrudgingly mumbles.

'There that wasn't difficult was it. Erminia will see you tomorrow,' Angela declares, feeling her mission accomplished.

'Get in.' Erminia ignores the limp gesture of the young woman she despises, but whose talent she recognises.

Angela refrains from suggesting they offer Jaysie a lift knowing winning one small battle is probably the extent of her current power of persuasion.

As the passenger door closes and before either have slipped into their seat belts, the wheels spin metaphorical dust over the statue that is her downcast sous chef.

They are well into their journey before either speak. Angela feels they have to clear the air on Jaysie and that it will be wrong to change the subject before doing so. She slips her hand onto Erminia's thigh and gently squeezes in an indication of shared warmth. Erminia continues to focus on the road not moving her hands from the wheel.

'She doesn't mean it nastily,' Angela says. ' She just wants to impress you.'

'Impress me, undermine me more like. Very soon she needs to get out from under my feet and get her own kitchen. I'm not crazy. Of course the secondi dish is superior, but that isn't the point, the idea is for me to show off the Magpie at its best. That's what'll bring the house down,' Erminia explains tersely.

'Yes but you haven't told her. She just thinks it's a fucking mushroom,' Angela says, annoyed at the ridiculousness of the situation.

There is some silence before Angela speaks again.

'She really does admire you Ermi. You need to cut her some slack.'

'You want me to tell her so she can go and announce it to the world?' Erminia asks, taking a bend too fast, sufficient to earn a finger from an oncoming cyclist.

'She wouldn't do that. She's okay,' Angela assures her, whilst stretching her neck to see if the cyclist has managed to maintain his balance.

'What is it with you and Jaysie?' Erminia turns her head and catches Angela's eye as she drives the question home. 'You think she's cute don't you. You trying to fuck her, is that it?'

'Christ Ermi, what's got into you she's almost a poppa,' Angela says indignant.

'Hardly, she's twenty three.'

'Yeah and I'm thirty eight,' she retorts, almost adding, *'...and nearly old enough to be her mother,'* but holds back not wanting to labour her own maturity .

The interior of the car is again given over to silence. Angela sorts through a wallet of CDs partly to occupy her hands and partly to find a sound they can share without bickering, but they arrive at the cottage before she selects something suitable to change the mood. Bianco is at the window, two feet up on the sill, the long stump of his docked tail furiously swishing. Erminia waves which signals to Bianco he should race round to the door. Walking through the garden, Erminia discreetly takes Angela's hand.

'Angie, I'm sorry. I don't know what's got into me recently. I guess this Magpie thing is stressing me more than I realise.'

'You can be such a fucking arse sometimes, Ermi you know that,' Angela says lifting her hand and kissing Erminia's.

At this point the conversation is interrupted as Angela turns the key in the lock and they both nearly hit the ground with Bianco's flying greeting. A white bundle in the air at waist height then on the gravel and a four feet spring into space. Bianco doesn't stop bouncing and they don't stop laughing.

o0o

Erminia is over the moon, she has been accepted as a contestant on The Professional Grande Saucier show and her one concern has proved to be without foundation. The show is scheduled to air live prime time in the fourth week of February, with rehearsals set for three days during the second week. The restaurant will be closed for the annual vacation so any issue relating to service under the sole supervision of Jaysie is of no concern. The disappointment surrounding Jaysie when this becomes apparent is pronounced. But taking Angela's council, Erminia seeks to champion the sous chef's knowledge and actions wherever the opportunity arises.

At the rehearsals, the cooking of the dish being judged will not be required. Ingredients may be brought and cooked to enable the chefs to test the ovens, salamanders, blast freezers and any other equipment they will be using. Decisions will be made on who will occupy which station and camera shots, sound tests, lighting, audio, heating affects will be walked through to ensure familiarisation. Rules, judging, disqualification criteria will be reinforced by the production company. On the day – no second chances, no multiple takes, one live performance, warts and all.

Leading up to the Christmas period il bar and De Regio are manic. Bookings for private functions are accepted in the restaurant for lunch, and much of each afternoon is spent on hands and knees picking up plastic compasses, manicure sets, dice and the other unwanted winnings of pulled crackers along with party popper containers that vacuum cleaners will not digest, while cleaners employed on extra shifts get the less sought after experience of cleaning the toilets and car park of undigested turkey with all the trimmings lubricated with over-priced De Regio branded champagne and jugs of bitter.

Angela makes several trips to America with designs she has sketched of possible pieces, and gets back from her last jaunt late on Christmas Eve with a bag load of presents scooped up from various New York temples of retail.

Christmas Day falls on a Monday so along with Erminia's policy that De Regio does not offer a Xmas lunch, there is no work. Angela and Erminia sleep in, eat brunch and walk Bianco. They read articles to each other from the weekend broadsheet glossies, listen to music, eat cold food bought in from the Lechmead deli and drink a little too much. The following morning, life begins again and before they know it the new year is already rolling into February.

o0o

Jaysie turns up for the rehearsal on time, coming from a few days staying with her parents who ten years previous had moved from Deptford into a house on a new development on the outskirts of Thetford, eighty miles north of London. With a huge forest on the back doorstep there, the sous chef had voiced an interest in probing for the possibility of a wider range of wild food than her boss has access to in Kent. With little opportunity for a long haul getaway this year, Jaysie took refuge in the forest whilst visiting her parents with whom she is attempting to build bridges over her sexuality.

Erminia is shocked at the number of people on set. Many it appears will be off camera, but even those who don't form part of the crew are substantial, plus there will be three judges whose identity will not be revealed until the shoot. There are ten contestants, all professional chefs and each may be accompanied by a personally selected Commis, who will not be permitted to cook. Their main duties being to run and fetch – they are sanctioned to prepare vegetables that will lose their shape, peeling and cutting potatoes for mashing being a case, but not sculpting vegetables that form part of the visual aspect of the finished dish. The Commis is also requested to stay out of shot wherever possible.

Fifty percent of the contestants, Erminia does not recognise, they would seem to be known less than she is, three she believes attract similar media exposure to herself and two have high profile celebrity status. Of the Commis Chefs she is amazed to see one is a previous winner of Master Chef who has since become a face on the Daytime TV sofas and in the tabloid press. Erminia has nominated Jaysie to support her, and she has accepted.

For the last few days prior to the big day, Jaysie is around almost constantly, tagging Erminia like an insecure puppy dog, but without making a nuisance of herself. In fact, Erminia finds having her around in some ways pacifying. With no other staff in sight, being completely alone could see her nerves begin to shred. The only thing Erminia is not prepared to allow is having her new shadow accompany her and Bianco on their early morning walks. It is only sometime later, Erminia recalls Jaysie's muddy boots trampling into the kitchen more than once.

Call time was for two hours before the start of programme. Erminia and Jaysie arrive thirty minutes ahead of schedule. Changing, makeup, signing a repeat of all the previous documentation, setting up. She notices all the other chefs are wearing head wraps or skull caps, but she wears a cut-down, starched white, tall, chef's hat. She feels this makes her stand out and maintain the classical look. She also wears a neckerchief, which she has noticed on many cooking programmes the chefs have dispensed with. Her chef's jacket is white, with a green and red De Regio motif embroidered above her left breast, and also on the back right shoulder, so it is also visible when she is walking away from camera. She feels good and she can see Jaysie is on her toes. Not all the contestants are as positive, she clocks a couple popping beta blockers to stop their hand vibrating, although she is not sure that this is allowed.

It is at this point the judges are paraded out and introduced. First, to a round of applause, is a man who looks like a pop star with flowing black hair taking on strands of grey. He fronts a TV show and is in the top handful of Sommeliers, along with membership of the Court Of Master Sommeliers. A palate few can surpass. Both the celebrity chefs give him a slight nod, which Erminia takes as acknowledgement of their previous acquaintance.

The second ushered on stage is a woman of slight demeanour who few would mark as the holder of two Michelin Stars. She is greeted with an equal coming together of hands and similar indications of recognitions from the celebrity chefs.

To Erminia's amazement the bull-frog of a man, the third judge brought out is Erminia's long-standing, valued customer who in his own inimitable style robustly thanks his audience for their approval albeit considerable less buoyant than for the two previous judges. He is introduced as a lesser known commentator within the gourmet arena, today representing the taste buds of the bon vivant, the paying epicurean – ha ha.

The celebrity chefs make no moves in favour of this arbiter, Erminia feels she should at least smile when he faces the competing chefs to give them a perfunctory clap for the contest on which they are about to embark. Erminia's smile is returned blank.

The dish in which the Baby Magpies will give prominence is cooked mushroom three ways, wild leaf of various species, crayfish sautéed in butter and flambéed with a Liqueur de Pamplemousse Rosé will also be included in the ingredients. Jaysie is tasked with cleaning, chopping and liquidising the baby magpies that will form the basis of a soft light jelly in which individual shreds of green leaf will be suspended and incorporated into a dark, rich coulis.

'I have prepared a little more than we discussed so you can taste and taste again without fear of being left with none to serve,' Jaysie tells Erminia smiling at the idea. She offers her the first teaspoon of the maceration. 'A little way to go yet.'

Erminia is not sure why she is being told this; they have practiced it so many times before that she imagines Jaysie knows it like the Lord's Prayer. But nerves affect different people in different ways. She seems very focused and is not displaying any cause for concern. Erminia tastes three more spoonfuls before the split is made. The seasoning for the coulis will be a distinctly more powerful reduction, the jelly lighter, let down before gelatine is added. Speed is now of essence if the preparation is to set in time. The addition of near frozen liquid and ice cubes to the mixture is her secret solution. Taste, cleanse palette, taste again. Everything must enhance, a smidgen too much and the 'Babies' will be killed. But all is fine, the presenter calls a time reminder. The Stage Manager is waving some of the Commis chefs out of shot, Erminia is pleased this has not been necessary for Jaysie, who is being an angel; performing well and behaving completely to brief. During rehearsals at the De Regio, the two have devised and learned a discreet form of sign language, so if Erminia is about to miss something Jaysie can alert her without the microphones picking it up. This is also proving successful.

Erminia had decided to make her revelation known to the world by announcing it during the chat that is undertaken by the presenter touring the kitchen when each contestant is interrogated in the course of the show. Ninety seconds is approximately scheduled for this chat. *What is the dish? What are the ingredients? How is the preparation being handled? What methods of cooking are being used? Why has this particular dish been chosen? Why do you think this combination of flavours will stun the judges and*

win you the accolade of Professional Grand Saucier of the Year?
At the last moment, halfway through the interview
Erminia changes her mind. After the presenter has
moved on to the next contestant she wonders if she
chickened out. Her decision now is to break the news
in front of the judges when she is called to place her
dish, three portions, on the table before them.

However, she is now experiencing a further
quandary. Let the cat out of the bag so to speak prior
to the silver spoons, shovelling the concoction into
their open mouthed but possibly closed minds. Judges
often want what they know, what they recognise, but
done better. The idea of judging something completely
new could prove rebarbative. Or she could wait until
the ingredients have been swallowed, comments made,
but then the concern escalates that the surprise of the
unidentifiable being overlooked might make the judges
feel stupid and alienate them from the contestant.
Nobody likes to be made to look foolish. Erminia is
worried the whole exercise could backfire. And she is
now beginning to feel nauseous.

She squeezes a spice grater, a sharp serrated cone
hardly bigger than a Baby Magpie, in the palm of her
hand, the metal does not cut her but is enough to pull
her thoughts from her dilemma to the pain.
Concentrate on presenting the best dish she tells
herself. From Jaysie a knife-tapping attention grabber,
a frown and gesture darts across to move her to the
next stage.

Back in the zone, she signs Jaysie to check the jelly,
it is still too wet, Erminia checks her watch, still time,
remove the panic from the equation. If the dish is not

finished it can't be presented and with that neither option will be available.

Taste, taste, taste, it's all about the taste. All the other chefs are plating. The aromas, even where oppugnant, mingle and light up Erminia's sensory synapses. There are only a few things that do this and most carry her back to the cobbled streets of her childhood.

Jaysie is frantically signing plate, plate, plate now.

Out of shot the judges have taken their places on the outer boundary of the set. Erminia's attention is stolen by the red light indicating a cut to the camera documenting their entrance. They sit, sombre smiles held at the ready.

Erminia is feeling sick. The stage manager is signalling with his fingers, three, the presenter calls it.

'Three. Three minutes and its over.'

A finger is closed down.

'Two. Two minutes. You have two minutes left. Everything should be on the plate,' the presenter warns.

Erminia's head is down, her fingers are working at speed, tweezers picked up, used, put down, tasting spoon taking up a final smear although it is now too late to adjust.

'One minute. One minute ladies and gentlemen.

Erminia glances over to Jaysie who is signalling encouragement with the circle of her thumb and forefinger. With her stomach churning she is looking around.

'That's it. Times up. Please step away from your bench.'

Erminia is the third to present. The first two receive high praise, little room to draw a blade between them, although each judge has found fault, no, dissenting opinion, which they attest is at the highest level. Nothing really. Erminia can see the competition is at the professional peak. But she will win. She looks down at her plate and knows it's perfect, but it will be her revelation that will be the crowning factor.

'Chef three, come forward please,' the presenter invites.

As practiced Erminia takes her first plate and the other two plates are brought to the judging trestle by a waiter who remains out of shot. Sweating, she is still undecided as to the moment of her announcement. She glances over to her station to seek Jaysie's encouragement, but all the Commis chefs have retired to the changing rooms.

'Judges, ladies and gentlemen before you taste my creation, I would like to announce to everyone present, our viewers and the rest of the world, that I have discovered a new ingredient, a mushroom never before recognised and never before documented. It is this mushroom, the Magpie Erminia Fungus, a dwarf *coprinus picaceus* which unlike it's bigger brother which is poisonous if eaten, the MEF used in this dish before you, can be eaten without any side effects whatsoever...'

The word *Enjoy!* does not make it to the end of the sentence. It is drowning. Coming from the bowels of the earth, everything, every morsel she has ever consumed is erupting from her mouth and through her nostrils, out in twelve-gauge shotgun spray, shrapnel immediately followed by golf ball looped trajectories.

She sees direct hits and multi coloured lubricant slopping down the face and shirt of the man heralded as the voice of the eating public. Erminia doubles, folding at her knotted gut over the table, feeling it begin to give under her weight, the white cloth, glasses, palette cleansers and her presentation dishes all tobogganing with increasing momentum to the floor. She can feel her anus relaxing. She is becoming an unpleasant oozing mass before six million viewers.

'Cut for fucks sake, cut camera four,' is being screamed into crew ear pieces. 'Go to camera two.'

PART TWO

Going to ground

CHAPTER FIVE

ME is at my elbow. I can feel the smooth skin manicure of his hand touching my skin. He is talking to the guests standing in front of me. Apologising on behalf of the restaurant. Apologising on my behalf. Apologising. I have a faint recollection of saying something insulting. Abusive. Possibly using the C-word, almost certainly using the F-word. Other diners, I assume are obfuscated, confused as to the wrangle they are witnessing; an exchange more reminiscent of the street corner at kicking-out time.

Reluctantly I do allow myself to be shepherded away, back towards the kitchen. I can hear a voice somewhere saying, *'Of course there'll be no charge, sir.'*

People are such absolute shits. I can remember it even at school. Kids. I wonder if it's a natural instinct or something learned. The need to be a 'me too', the shared experience, the need to gather the empathy in, to feed off someone else's trouble, some unpleasant episode. I don't remember the same with good things.

Did no-one want to receive the praise of an event that brought joy? Maybe they did and I just never noticed.

My mother had got a large splinter in her leg while working in the orchard and I had had to go to the farmacia, or my nonna had missed her bus to come and stay with us and I had needed to wait until the next one as I had promised my mother I would carry her mother's bags from the stop to our house. I don't recall the problem, it could have been either or neither. Whatever it was the little girl who sat in the front row of my school class made incessant stabs at the ceiling to gain attention and brag to the teacher that this is what had happened to her, but earlier and the splinter was of course bigger or the grandmother much older, much frailer. The bags were twice the size. Now it was happening here, here in De Regio.

I'm back in my office, pouring another glass of whatever it is I'm drinking now. Jaysie is standing in the doorway.

'There was nothing wrong with any of those plates,' Jaysie sounds as hurt as I feel.

I nod in agreement and offer her a glass, which she refuses. I pull the cork on a fresh bottle regardless. I'm tired, I've drunk too much for a lunchtime. I've drunk too much full stop. This has been going on for three months now. Since the day I puked over six million. Tired, not physically, just mentally exhausted from fighting to retain or more re-establish my position in the market. De Regio's name. The alcohol is just a clear reflection of the fact that I'm pissed off.

Many nights I get a taxi home, too pissed to drive. Other nights I drive anyway.

The shower is now a place for washing away the sweat and the smell of booze that seems to constantly ooze from my pores, the aroma of the last gallon of whatever it was I had selected, although selected is probably the wrong word. The first time I have any recognition of the vintage is as it swirls in the mist. In some ways I feel this a comfort. Reassuring. Angela is angry with me, I know. I can't remember the last time we had sex and she is being demanded to attend meetings in New York more and more. When she's away, Bianco is getting neglected, but does not seem to mind. He still comes to the gate to greet me, regardless of my state or the hour.

Every morning Bianco still accompanies me to a patch to pick, but more and more I know I'm paranoid. Plants I would have picked without a second thought, I now find I check on an app on my phone. When there is no signal, I err on the side of caution.

Sometimes I think I lie to myself – not every morning, but more often than not. When we don't go, Bianco makes do with prowling the garden and De Regio makes do with what remains in the cold room from the previous service or if busy, rarer than ever was once the case, I buy in and pay an extortionate charge for immediate courier delivery – biked over from the other side of nowhere. I've begged and borrowed from other establishments once or twice. Chefs can be sympathetic.

oOo

Three months have passed since the day it all started to fall apart, but perhaps I've already said that.

All across the papers. Not just the Locals, Nationals too, even some of the foreign press carried the picture. Tabloids went for front pages; broadsheets didn't ignore it either albeit tucked discreetly nearer the middle. Image trending on Twitter, You Tube, #vomitapproach went viral. Famous for fucking it up. Chucking it up.

Some of the customers remained loyal. Some came to eat, but confirmed that six months ago they had had a bad experience the following day. Their grannies bags were heavier, the shard of timber in their leg was longer, sharper. Recipes using ingredients not cultivated under controlled conditions were highly suspect. Why hadn't Health and Safety clamped down or was it Environmental Health? They didn't know but someone should have stopped it.

'Yes, I've been drinking but what's that to you. If you don't like the food why come back. And anyway I don't think you've ever been here before anyway. Fuck. Fuck. Fuck. Lady why don't you just go down the road and eat some tasteless battery chicken pumped full of steroids and poisoning millions of people with campylobacter and other shit.' I think I remember spitting that out at some point early on.

I don't think I remember backhanding her iPhone across the restaurant as she stepped away to Instagram more unpalatable evidence of what I'm not sure. But they say I did.

Good wine is better than bad wine, but any wine is better than no wine. I moved down market when Angela screamed at me for drinking the profits.

Some days were worse than others, the worst was when I held fast, tried to remain the person I was, barked on the pass, tasted sauces before they left while trying to ignore the fungus growing on my tongue. Within a month two chefs had left, the candidates from the application pending stack didn't pick up when called or had miraculously secured positions in unnamed three star Michelin kitchens. Commis chefs were promoted. The PR company set out campaigns, in which it was becoming clear even to my blurred vision I was nowhere to be seen.

Christ I throw up. So fucking what. Deep down I think I was depressed.

Monday Monday, great song Mamas and Papas or would be if I could remember if it is Monday. Halfway to De Regio, when John Humphreys alerts me to the fact, is when I realise what day it is. I've turned round and come back. Bianco is in the garden and I'm in the kitchen drinking a very dry craft cider from the can and cooking breakfast on the stove rather than over an open fire.

'What in fucks name are you doing here?' I demand of Jaysie.

My sous chef is in the garden using a black poo bag to pick up a mound of Bianco's shit. The dump he was expecting to have down by the river.

'I didn't know you were around,' Jaysie replies half startled.

Liar liar pants on fire. I don't say it but the smell even in the garden of my sizzling bacon can't be missed and certainly not mistaken especially by a chef even with poo bag in hand

'Whether I'm around or not, I don't get it. What're doing here?' Is what I am saying.

'Angie asked me to pop by each day while she's away. Make sure the dog didn't get neglected.'

I throw the can I'm still holding at her. It is not empty, but I am not begrudging the loss. It misses and Bianco bounds off across the lawn, teeth piercing the thin aluminium, joining me in my early day livener – although I know he leans towards a dark bitter.

Jaysie brushes off the liquid that has sprayed across her shoulder. I had been aiming for her head.

'You need to get to work, before you haven't got job,' I am telling her, although it is six hours before her shift is due to start which I know but it doesn't stop me.

'It's you that'll be out on your arse before I am.'

I whistle, spraying cider spit as I call Bianco in.

'He's not the dog, he's Bianco,' I am adding as we, that's me and Bianco, head into the house. At this moment I am deciding to not call Jaysie chef anymore, just Jaysie. Reverse panegyric.

It is Monday, so my knowledge of Jaysie's shift not starting for another six hours is also wrong. Twenty-four plus six. Thirty hours. Time for her carry out another invasion into my life. I am half a mind to go out to one of Angela's favourite restaurants and have a good lunch alone. But I only drink and drive when I need to get home. I don't start off with that notion. Besides sitting in the middle of someone else's eatery being gawked at by staff, smiled at in a ridiculous manner by customers and, and, and… I've thought this before, I seem to recollect…

I open a can of Tanglefoot, which has no designated reason to be around, except maybe being held in abeyance for a beef and ale something or a beer batter. I glug some of the brown fizzy liquid into Bianco's bowl, we can get pissed together. What were Monday's made for?

It's dark and a lot of cider later, when I see the De Regio come into view. Bianco is or was when I left, asleep on the sofa. Comatosed. I decided to walk, but now I'm here I can't remember the cause of my venture. Cinnamon I think, but that can't be right as I can see some in the spice rack. I think I'm cooking a lamb tagine.

I am being helped up by a member of the local constabulary, a second one takes my other arm. They recognise me from adverts in the regional press or horror of horrors… TV.

The damage I've caused is to my own property and the forced entry, in which lays the consequence of the alarm destroying the peace is also within my personal ownership. So no charges.

Returning the High Street to silent mode takes the best part of forty minutes. Every time I get up I step through the space that is my body. Not chalked out but defined by white broken china and other dining paraphernalia that has been brought crashing to the floor as I'd tumbled and stumbled in my race to smash my face on the floor boards. Aberfan, a negative view, but why this has slipped into my consciousness I have no idea, 1966, 144 dead, 116 kids. Before I was even born for Christ sake. Must have been an anniversary. I give the cops a bottle of spirit each and they give me a ride home.

Against all the rules but better that than wasting another hour on the shout that would be inevitable. Safely banged up at home, I dispense with Morocco, pour myself and Bianco more alcohol which having more sense than me he avoids.

There is a bottle of something hard, now empty, which I do not recall as being a liquid I have consumed. A cool draught gives me the shivers which indicates I have again without recall opened the back door into the garden. Bianco is barking. My head is banging. I stumble around searching drawers for tablets that will remove the Jamaican steel band from between my ears. I need to clear up, but the thought of bending over to collect the packaging of my private party is more than I can contemplate. I decide to shower before dressing for work. I must have a shift starting soon. I sit naked in the tiled shower pan then with even concerted stretching with arms that may not be mine, realise I can't reach the tap without getting up. I pee and fall asleep.

'Christ this place smells worse than some downtown back alley.'

I've woken up. The steel band have not packed up and gone.

'Emi are you here?'

I am not answering. Yes might be a lie.

'Jaysie… Jaysie? Is that you?'

I guess she has heard the shower curtain coming part way down as I try to pull myself to my full height but without making it. Jaysie does not answer. Not here either. Or maybe she is. Asleep in my bed. Little fucking Red Riding Hood. She's probably eaten the porridge too. Little shit.

Angela is furious. Her face is stone. I am going to tell her it looks like one of her more twisted effigies. But I know what's good for me and I know I'm in the wrong. She grabs Natalie Wood by the hair and badly hooks the curtain back in place although most of the fastenings have torn away and then turns the water on. On full. Power shower. I guess I'm lucky it is not on boiling or ice cold; she does not make to test the temperature. Now I'm on my own, except for Natalie who is drowning in running water. I wonder if it is not insensitive manufacturing shower curtains with her face on them.

The note reads *Have taken B for a walk. Get the place cleaned up.* That is it. No signature. No love.

I do as I have been instructed.

Everything is bagged and binned including the missive. I do this naked. I think if I go into the bedroom to get clothes I will ignore everything and take to my bed. Our bed. Vacuuming is beyond the call of duty, the noise will be there to herald the return of the Jamaicans that can't have gone far, only departing with the deluge of water. On my hands and knees, I brush.

Angela and Bianco do not return until an hour after I have returned the place to some sort of normality. I am dressed, wearing an overcoat and sitting in the garden. It is far from warm but I feel the need for fresh air.

I won't repeat the conversation we are having. It is all one-sided. Angela does not tell me about herself or her trip, everything is about me. I agree to the demands. Why wouldn't I. All that is being demanded is that I return this body, which has been infiltrated by bad behaviour to Erminia. Naturally I promise I will.

We are sleeping on opposite sides of the bed. I need a hug but do not know how to ask. In the morning, Angela goes straight to fire up the forge which I have allowed to go out and I go straight to the restaurant. It's been three days, apparently. Foraging can wait another.

'My kids didn't get their dinner money this week. They had to make do with a packet of crisps each. Do you think that's acceptable.'

It wasn't a question.

'While you're there cooking your fancy food my kids are going hungry.'

'I'm sorry Mr Jones, if you'd like to pop round now I can square up with you. I haven't been well,' I tell him.

'Your woman sent me a cheque. I haven't been there for a week, so you owe me nothing now. And I've got another job… where they pay me.'

The phone goes dead in my hand.

Mr Jones is, was, the gardener, not that there is a garden. He kept the car park clean, the plant pots in good order and stood in for the KP when he was off or we were exceptionally up the wall. It's 11 a.m., I've been in for a couple of hours. When I arrived, the car park looked as though one of our bins had been emptied out in it. Picking everything up and making it look like somewhere it would be nice to arrive at is the next job on my list. I could wait and ask the Kitchen Porter to do it, but he doesn't get in until two hours after service in il bar has kicked off.

I am half way through filling the second black bag when the postman pulls in and hands me a stack of envelopes that are more bills, to join the allotted piles Angela yesterday placed neatly in some sort of order on my desk. When I've cleared up this mess, I'll see what needs doing with that.

The Margate émigré will not arrive for another half hour, so I go behind the bar and help myself. I choose a craft ale, something clean and refreshing will do the trick, I have a thirst on par with the pyramids, but I go for the bottle that's the largest. It's cold and when I've downed it I need another, but it is now that I remember my promise and stop myself. Promises are there to be broken but I've already managed that. Tom is in when I get back into the kitchen and he actually looks pleased to see me.

The full time kitchen and restaurant staff are all on fixed wages and paid by standing order, so they're all looked after. However, going through the bank statement, two that have left have still been getting paid. Fat chance of getting that back. The balance is low. The cost of running the place is not being covered by the customer spend. It does not take a visit to the accountant to figure out that it is the takings from il bar that is keeping the business afloat.

Next to me on the desk is a cup of coffee and a glass of water, neither of which seem to be a substitute for the second bottle of beer I did not take.

I go through the suppliers' invoices and the total will wipe out the overdraft and then some. But if I can stagger the payments and the rest of the week is not too bad, I think I can save the day. I need to get back in the game.

I come home quite early, everything is closed and locked up by ten. Eleven covers on a Friday night. Lunchtime at il bar was better. The atmosphere around the staff individually is varied, but the overall feel is distant.

In bed our bodies are touching but not with any passion, just not jumping away each time we cannon. I have not been drinking, the first time in weeks (except for the one beer downed before I remembered I was off it).

Saturday night is better and Sunday lunch is acceptable. On both days I have foraged with Bianco, although I have avoided even the thought of going to the Baby Magpie site. The idea of using the term MEF is more abhorrent to me than anything else I can imagine.

On Monday Angela, Bianco and I are somewhat our usual selves. That is to say Angela is not making detours into rooms she has no business in when the appearance of us meeting up seems likely. A ridiculous strategy in a country cottage. I cook, meals are served without wine, Angela's concession to my fight for abstinence. No sex though. Our distance in bed does not seem physical.

Dandelion and burdock roots have formed much of this Tuesday mornings forage. Bianco is running and chasing squirrels and I am savouring my favourite rashers with sourdough French toast. Munching away with the strongest appetite I've had since the TV fiasco, I am planning in my head how I can rebuild De Regio's business, my reputation, the credibility of cooking with wild food and at the same time revamp my love life.

'Bianco… Bianco,' I call and call again. He's nowhere in sight and seemingly turning a deaf ear.

Back at the Defender, he is still missing. I put him his breakfast down, add a bowl of fresh water and use the whistle. Where he came from I'm not sure but before I stop blowing he's here standing behind me, like he's been there all the time.

oOo

'What the fuck's this? I'm shouting at a woman who's fault I know it's not. She's just a body with an iPad hanging around in the foyer, discouraging customers from beating up machines that dispense cash in unwanted denominations, fail to have sufficient paper to issue receipts for monies being deposited or from standing in a lengthening queue in front of the single cashier that was, up until a few weeks ago, the workload of three. I push the letter at her face, poke, poke, poke. She is looking away, pleading with the camera hanging from the ceiling.

I allow myself to be shepherded into a cubicle when a man in a cheap somewhat fluffy suit appears.

'I want to speak to the manager, the business manager,' I demand, then clarify.

'I'm sorry that's not possible, he's only here on Monday and Friday,' The iPad carrying lady explains as she tries to leave me in the new hands to return to customers venting their disappreciation on machines that are underperforming and can't fight their corner.

'You might be able to speak to him on the inter-branch phone if he is not with a client,' she offers, but I want to poke out someone's eyes.

I'm offered coffee, brown, made with less than hot water served in a paper cup, probably at this temperature so the drinker has no excuse for remaining longer than it takes for three gulps. I refuse. I've already experienced puking over the public once and that didn't go well.

My accountant, flushed, comes in through the front door, which automatically opens at a slower pace than his stride causing him to perform a dance step I do not recognise. He looks around and is nodded in my direction by iPad woman.

Outside, bloodshot mist vision is the result of my fury, but does not in any way amount to the level of apoplectic rage I am displaying and that is less than I'm experiencing. My accountant is walking me to his car, a big thing; my eyes can't focus on the make or the colour, which certainly is tinged with red.

'I tried to call-by before the post arrived, they sent me a PDF copy over. I wanted to warn you it was on it's way.'

I get out the car in which I had hardly had time to sit, kick the passenger door as I am striding away.

'He fucking knew. They'd probably fucking discussed it before it was even written. Asshole. I never trusted him.' I am talking to myself. I might even be talking to you, if I fucking knew who you are.

Jaysie is in the kitchen talking to Tom as I come in tearing the letter withdrawing De Regio's overdraft with immediate effect and demanding full repayment before… before they drive me into bankruptcy… which will probably be in the next half hour.

I am telling them there is no point in opening, there is no money to buy stock or pay wages. They are not speaking, just staring at me as if I have just come from some alien world… which I suppose is as near to the truth as it gets.

Jaysie speaks. 'A has sent over some cash, enough to cover the salaries and buy whatever we need to keep the doors open.'

Now it's me that's not speaking.

I throw the letter in the air and don't stay to watch it float in multiple rocking motions before landing largely in the friture. Before leaving, I fill a bag with a selection of Grand Cru and a bottle of XO, which I am chugalugging as I make the car park and head for home. I am not bringing my stash in, I move it from the Jag into the Defender.

'You fucking knew before I did… I can't believe it… You didn't have the balls to even warn me…' I am screaming at her. Bianco has gone into hiding at the top of the house or behind the shed or wherever he goes when he wants to get away.

'I did what needed doing. Not ranting and raving… I did what you should have been doing, not caterwauling all over town.'

I take a bottle of beer from the fridge, flick the top and down it at a speed that sends froth out of the corners of my mouth, which as I lick it back in tastes salty from the tears streaming down my cheeks.

'And you can stop the drinking. Take control of yourself and the business. I've got enough on my plate without doing your job. If I wanted to run a restaurant I'd be running my own not running yours which I've virtually been doing since…'

Angela has stopped now. I grasp the fact she is exasperated with me but she just doesn't get it. I take another beer from the fridge down it and am walking out.

oOo

It must be Monday, the restaurant is not open and there is nobody here. I've been drinking but I'm not wrecked. It dawns on me that it may not be Monday and De Regio has in fact closed down. Ceased trading. I think I was in a train crash some days back and the small amount I'm drinking now is just to make me feel better. It is at this moment the answer hits me square in the face. The problem is the F word. As of now, no more foraging. Rebuild on the reputation of high-end produce, the Grand Cru of produce. Everyone's fucking terrified I'm going to pick something unbelievable that's going to end up tearing their guts out.

I am deciding it must be Monday, filtering through clogged grey stuff, I am getting a distant memory, like being in college or church, maybe a police caution but it is none of those. A's voice, giving the lecture on her doing what it was she thought I should be doing. What she had done. And what I'm comprehending is that she will not have let the operation go under.

The alcohol I'm drinking now is clearing my head, a dry cider, not too dry, is what I fancy at this second, and that should do it. I can see you, whoever you are, out there frowning. Reading. Well frown so more. I walk through to il bar and open what I think comes close. I told you, I don't need your black looks and if you open your mouth, it's over, I'll stop right now and then you'll never know how this ends.

CHAPTER SIX

I'm awake now, laying in bed. Drowsy. I recognise the
pattern on the duvet so deduce I am in my own bed
and as clarity begins to return to my eyes, I see the wall
coverings, the paintings, the drapes and the furniture
to confirm this. I can see, but there is a dimness. It is
possible there is a night-light on somewhere although I
have no recollection of there being one, except for
bedside lamps and it is not either of those. I am
wondering how I feel but there is nothing. I check to
see if my limbs are still attached but nothing moves
and they are hidden under the covers. I have said I am
checking but this is not the interpretation of the truth
– along with my arms and legs, my head I also can't
lift. An unseeable weight has me pinned down. I can
feel it now, heavy, pressing me, my whole torso, my
whole being, into the mattress. I'm scared. I'm fighting
it, I am a warrior with no weapons. All my defences
are down. I am screaming without sound escaping.

This is all too much.

o0o

I'm awake now, laying in bed. Drowsy. I recognise the pattern on the duvet so deduce I am in my own bed and as clarity begins to return to my eyes, I see the wall coverings, the paintings, the drapes and the furniture to confirm this. Daylight, not bright, not summer's day glare, but sufficient to fill the room. I roll over. It is dawning on me I have moved. I speak to myself, quietly but out loud. '*I hear you,*' I tell myself. In the future, I will tell a physician of my earlier ordeal, which at this moment I can recall vividly and imagine it to have been some death stage I was passing through.

I get out of bed and begin to wander. There is no sound apart from the sounds I am making. Footfalls, opening a door, hinge squeaking, latch clicking, stairs creaking, my own breathing.

On the kitchen table I can see a note written in felt tip. Angela has gone. She will be back in three days. Bianco has been put into kennels; I should say at this stage, I am devastated, this is not an experience he has every before been required to endure. All alcohol has been removed from the cottage and the car keys confiscated. The larder has been fully stocked. The doctor apparently administered me a sedative and has left a bottle of tranquillisers or similar which I should take as per the directions on the label. She is sure I will be able to take care of myself as long as I take these and stay off the booze.

I've been up a few hours and I'm still pissed that Bianco is banged up, mixing with who knows who in some home for the unloved. All the other things I am putting to one side or dealing with as solutions present.

There is one other piece of information that I am now coming to realise; I have been left without money and my credit cards have mysteriously vanished. This has not been scrawled in large blue syllables by my keeper's finger on the tablets of parchment. This is not exactly the phrase I was taught in scuola di catechismo; *written by the finger of God on tablets of stone* rings a biblical bell but the feeling felt reminiscent. How many wasted hours, keeping children from under their mothers' aprons while the Sunday meal was being cooked. The church happy to crèche in exchange for the opportunity to drip, drip, drip their guilt-laden creed into the next generation.

Jesus never wanked I suppose.

Fuck Jesus, fuck the tablets, regretfully Bianco will have to bear his own cross until Angela can pay to roll away the stone, I am going back to work. Walk it I must. Walk it I will.

Tom is clearing down and Jaysie is gearing up. Tom is saying he is pleased to see me looking better, which I am of a mind to believe, and it is nice to see me back in the kitchen, which I am less inclined to believe. Jaysie with purely body language is openly hostile.

The first thing I do is put all Jaysie's trappings of a position she does not hold into a plastic bowl from the wash-up and deposit it on the pass for her to store in her locker, on her own time. This enhances her annoyance, adding to the attitude of her physical presence as she dust devils from one end of the kitchen to another.

'I don't know why you're so pissed off. The office is mine and there were plenty of unwashed bowls I could have used.' I do not say this, or anything else. The next thing I do is rewrite the dinner menu. It utilises no greenery, roots or other uncontrolled substances obtained at the cost of personal labour only. Just bought in, which I order now on the phone, cash on delivery as credit has been withdrawn from the usual suppliers and is not available from those I have never used before. Payment will be courtesy of a bundle of notes in the desk draw, no doubt due to Angela's civility.

As I pin the sheet to the menu board, Jaysie is peering over my shoulder.

'No way,' she shouts directly in my ear, 'that goes against everything we do. The cold room is stuffed with wild ingredients. I spent the whole of Monday driving up to Thetford picking it. My day off. No. I'm just not going to cook it. I did the menu before you could even get yourself in and that's what I'm doing, so you can go fuck yourself.'

I'm shaking my hand, it hurts, but not as much as Jaysie's jaw. She is oscillating on the floor, her head narrowly missed the corner of a working surface, so she's lucky. She went down like an iced Rolling Rock on a steaming hot day. Maybe I should buy a punch bag, take my frustrations out on that because I sure felt an uplift as she went down.

I'm sitting in A&E handcuffed to a fifteen year old, with the stature of a kid of ten. I vaguely remember them dropping the height restriction, but the age waiver alludes me. The swelling is increasing by the hour, yes I've been here hours. It must be getting close to his bedtime. Broken ankle is my guess. My knuckle is faring better. Some guy who's shit-faced sitting on the other side of the waiting area, that is actually not that busy, keeps staring at me. I have the inclination that if I could walk, crawl maybe, I'd go over there and bash him. They call my name while I'm making plans.

'How did it happen?' Well I can tell you I'm not admitting to anything. But so it's clear and there can be no misunderstanding, I bent down, face close to Jaysie, which was a stupid thing to do because it brought me in reach of her lashing out. I shouted, my face almost touching hers. I told her she was sacked, to get out, to fuck off and this time not to come back because next time I see her in my kitchen I'll cut her face off. Then for good measure, like so she doesn't think I'm joking I kick her in the head. Well that's what I intended, but she twists away at the moment of impact. The three-cornered stainless steel leg of the bain marie is even less forgiving than her thick skull.

I think she called the police. Someone did. I'd downed a fair amount of neat spirit, just to kill the pain – an act that most would appreciate was not unwarranted or OTT, before the flashing lights pulled up outside. Naively I assumed this to be an ambulance. Some thoughtful person realising I needed to be cared for.

I wake up being offered a breakfast tray, it tastes like porridge but it's not. The pain-killers are well into having worn off, hand and foot throbbing. I'm in one of the station cells. One in, one out. I hope he will leave in a better condition than me. I'm being told I will not be charged as a friend has persuaded the assaulted person not to press charges. Angela's back. Back in control. But I will be cautioned.

I tell him caution should be thrown to the wind and accompany this with an audible scoreggia.

Outside there is a taxi waiting to take me to the cottage. I go.

Angela is waiting as I arrive. The cuddle I am being given and the return I am delivering is without compromise. Bianco has survived without physical destruction. His tongue is all over my face. Finally for want of breath I am pushing him away and turn my attention to the schoolmistress standing in the corner of the room. The contact here is only verbal and it is getting straight to the point.

'I've shut the bar and the restaurant,' she is telling me. Matter of fact.

'That's not your decision,' I say, with what I consider to be unwarranted restraint.

'My decision, your decision, what's the difference. You've got no staff. Everyone's left you. Except me that is and you don't seem to give that much value. Tom has written you a very nice letter. More than you deserve. He said in the future if you can get your act together he would be pleased to give you a job, anytime'

She is handing an opened ivory coloured envelope to me.

'So you're reading my mail now,' I rebut.

'Someone's got to, because you certainly don't.'

I am walking away, into the kitchen. I open the fridge, it is clear of all alcoholic beverages. I settle for fizzy water. But I am discarding this before even breaking the seal on the cap. I don't really mind the lack of booze. I'm just doing this to give myself time to think.

'I've opened a new bank account and transferred some money into it. I've booked you into a detox clinic that an American friend of mine recommended and I've asked the PR company to prepare an relaunch strategy for later in the year. Once you're back on track we can run the place together and if that goes well you can become a signatory on the bank. A car will pick you up in the morning, please don't get pissed tonight.'

'What American friends have you got?'

This is the only thing I can think of saying at this moment.

The question goes unanswered. I put Bianco on a leash and walk out into the lane. I need to get out. Bianco is rarely in a position of restraint; it is not something he likes much, but is happy to be included despite stair-rods of rain targeting us with every step. For my part, each hit is making me feel alive. A cleansing of sort that is going far below the surface. Bianco is simply starting to look like a drowned rat.

oOo

The clinic looks like a cross between a public school and a mental asylum, set in grounds without barbed wire but more than overkill in the CCTV department. I guess someone is watching screens 24/7. Crazy. I guess some more and decide most of the inmates are public school and most of the staff are the crazies.

I can't recall how I spent the night after drying out. Bianco was towelled and then given a warm blow with the hairdryer to finish him off. I definitely had a port and brandy to take the chill away or that was my intention. But other than that most of the time between my walk in the rain and my walk up the stone steps of this dire place some days ago is less than a blur. I have some recollection of being met by a receptionist who checked me in with more efficiency than most four star hotels. And assured me of an ISO accreditation, and verified outcomes of the treatment programme provided by the clinic. She may have had a German or Austrian accent, but that might have been my imagination. I have not seen her since so verification remains elusive. Painting by numbers, swimming lengths, pumping iron and something to do with horse therapy I was also proudly informed was available to me. My en-suite room was also more spacious than most four star hotels. I did notice the fragrance of blooms in the foyer, which I believe was pumped in to mask a slight hospital aroma that pervaded the corridors the deeper one peregrinated into the bowels of this self-imposed abstinence. Not that it was my choice, a fact I'm sure has not slipped by unnoticed by anyone.

I have vague flashes, recurring memories, of being interrogated by a psychopath in a white coat sitting behind a desk. I sure I may have been diagnosed suitably to be drugged up with Benzos, not due to my excessive addiction but for my extreme disruptive tendency.

I overheard someone saying *I'd prefer to have a bottle in front of me than a frontal lobotomy* I conjure up this as being a quote attributed to John Wayne but I could be wrong. I give thought to the premise that Benzos is a chemical lobotomy but this could also be wrong.

I have come to understand my period of isolation from the real world has been set at twenty-eight days. This is based, I'm assuming, on the level of credit card payment offered up by my guardian Angel(a). In my head I have put brackets around the lower carriage first letter of the alphabet last letter of the figment. I am in here, the credit card payment is my key and thinking this I am recalling a Buddhist aphorism, *the keys to heaven also open the gates of hell.* Is it possible that heaven and hell are actually the same place? I ponder. To a Salvation Army-ist this could be paradise, to a sommelier - or a drunkard - pure hell? I ponder further. Could this mean God has a split personality? One day devil, one day saviour. As time goes by and the reality of life contrived becomes apparent, does the Almighty grow in crankiness? Could this explain why half the world is hungry and the other half obese. Half burning desert, half freezing tundra. A simple experiment. Do some creations receive a placebo? As I have no belief in God, I waste my time no further. I am heading out through open French windows across which gossamer nets are enthusiastically heralding total surrender. I have taken it into my head unannounced and unbooked, which I can imagine will provoke a bilious reaction in the German guardian of the gate, to investigate the ins and outs of horse therapy.

oOo

I am singing out loud, top of my voice, '...*walking back to happiness*' the Helen Shapiro 60's hit. Why I'm not clear because I don't think that's where I'm heading. I've been on the road for some sixteen hours, sticking to footpaths. The timing could be off, I had to hand over my watch and other valuables on checking in. The words of *Hotel California* starts to earworm, but I have left. Possibly it is the bird on the breeze overhead that has brought it swirling in, but I think it is a buzzard. I think of my steely knives and realise I'm homesick for my kitchen. It dives to prey and the Mama's and Papa's line earworms me. Monday, Monday. *What is going on in my head?*

I'm am not crazy. I checked out the horses, each stabled, some hoofing the doors (stay away from that – I move my thought on quickly) anyway they looked as if they needed therapy less than I do.

A police car pulled up alongside me a few hours back, they said they had been asked to keep an eye out for me, that I might be in distress. I assured them I wasn't, that the bill has been paid up fully to the end of the month and that I had no wish to return. They offered me a lift back and I again told them I did not wish to return, so they went on their way.

Formulating in the back of my brain is a plan. The drive from the cottage had lasted the best part of three hours. It was going to take more than the recommended 10,000 steps a day if I am not to be home this side of never.

I sleep out two nights and to my astonishment it feels quite good. Cold is the enemy, 4 a.m. is the killer time. The first night I bedded down late, so come four I had not slept much before the chill took to my bones. On the second night, I stretched out much sooner and slept through. Any warmth in the days was still apparent in the atmosphere early on, that was my reasoning, but there were other factors. The previous night I had opted for the bench seat in a rural bus shelter, staying off the ground was attractive but I think this enhanced the flow of cold air circulating around my lightly clothed torso. I tucked my hands in my pants which helped, another help may have been I was completely knackered from minimal sleep the night before. My bed for this kip was creeper I pulled down off a wall that seemed to circulate a large private estate, at one point I was concerned that the state of the decaying red bricks would fall with the loss of what was effectively webbing. But it didn't and the ivy retained a springiness and gave small pockets of air which my body heat was able to warm. On reflection, I think I should have considered sleeping during the day and walking at night, allowing the blood to flow during the coldest periods. But without a torch it would have meant walking on the road and in the dark. With loads of nutters about, I would have been diving for cover every time headlights lit the road. A full moon would have maybe been the best, rambling across fields without a tell-tale spot. But the season did not offer this up to me for consideration.

oOo

Opening the gate at the cottage, feeling pleased to be home, but then not. A quandary. Is this heaven or is this hell? I push The Eagles out of my mind and am unnerved by the lack of any attack from the bundle that is Bianco. I search my pockets for keys that I do not have. I have left my belongings at the loony bin, although I don't think I would have not kept valuables on my person. Everything in a place like that is currency. Keys to empty pads being passed on to unsavoury friends returned surreptitiously after the pickings were finished. Who were the greatest culprits I consider.

I go to the shed, the forge is cold, not lit for days, no embers, deprived of all heat. Completely unworked in days. Although my bones are cold and my joints aching, the shed still has much to offer up. Not my MEF's; they're are long gone. Hanging above their place is a large ham, dry curing. I have a faint recollection of Angela saying Jaysie had asked if she could drop it over and hang it there. I take it. I don't know what I'm thinking, but I feel it's something I am going to want. Under a flagstone Angela has a *safe* which once you know it is there, is not safe at all. In this hidey-hole is a can with cash in it, notes. When the deliveries of coke and iron arrive, they like to be paid in cash. Dirty and in work clothes Angela finds it easier to have money on hand. I take enough for what I have in mind. It does not seem to make sense not to take it all, but I don't. Keys, spare sets are also secreted away here.

In the cottage I take a few bits and pieces, not sufficient to alert Angela that I have been there. And as she does not appear to have any sculptures in progress I estimate it will be a while before she realises the safe has been rifled.

What I want her to feel is abandoned, abandoned like I have felt for months. Abandoned like Bianco must feel. I search everywhere for any papers relating to kennels, the one he has been lost to or even any that she may have viewed. Nothing. Maybe I'm being harsh. Maybe she has gone somewhere and taken him with her. But I do not believe this. All three vehicles are parked up, so she left by taxi, which is the usual modus operandi for an airport check-in.

I take the Jag, drive into town and get a complete set of keys cut – expensive. How can they warrant money like that for a two-minute job on a lathe I ask myself. There's no skill. It's just a copy.

Now I am driving to one of my secret spots, twenty-five miles away. Well, that's a lie but pretty close. In a woodland, with Private signs all over the place is an beaten and abused old caravan, used and owned I presume by an ageing couple of hippies I have spied over time coming and departing. They're not around much and never at this time of the year. I drop off everything I have bought and stash it under a tarp, which I cover with branches. I'm going to sleep in the caravan but should anyone turn up I don't want it to look as if I've moved in. This completed, I give the place a quick glance to check no telltale signs are screaming at me, leave a magpie of the bird variety guarding and drive back to the cottage. Dumping the car, I give the place the once-over and begin my walk. In town, I jump on a bus going in a direction opposite to my destination. It's a detour, with a purpose.

I'm not sure but I remember seeing an advert in the local paper, it must have been at least a year ago, so they could have gone to the wall by now, however when I get there they are still trading and open for business. I buy the cheapest second-hand bike they've got. They are not keen on selling it to me; well in truth they want the opportunity of doing it up before it goes. The requirement of now and no money is my argument against this. The no money wins the day; the deciding factor.

If I cycle hard I can be back at the caravan before dark, which as I am displaying no lights is a plus. There are two factors that may prevent my success, one the general roadworthiness of the bike itself and secondly, that I have not been on two wheels since leaving Italy and then not for a while before that. The whole thing is very shaky. I'm imagining the Tour de France during a Richter Scale 8. Horns of trucks blasting me as they go by do not enhance my stability. The idea of pedaling over dried mud footpaths will, I conclude, destroy either me or my purchase, or both. The last number of miles will need to be walked. Dismounting I can hardly put one foot in front of the other. I rest even though I am losing the light, and in the knowledge my muscles will seize. I do it regardless.

It is dark and the tree-cover blocks out the little light from the night sky that may be available out in the open. My eyes have become accustomed to the dark as I lean the bike frame against the rear of the van. I crouch, a foot on the high cross bar – it was a boys bike that was the purchase – and my knee on the saddle, and using a piece of stick I am with a certain amount of success able to lever open the back window. The catch is rotten, but so is the rest of it. I don't want the window to fall out, simply to allow it to open sufficiently for me to use my plinth to roll through. Inside, I am hoping the door can be unlatched and I will be able to bring in the supplies I will want day by day. I am now thinking ten days and then sneak back to see if Angela has returned, ever hopeful my absence has focused her mind and we can recreate 'us'.

The lock can't be disengaged without a key and despite a search under the mat, in coffee and tea caddies and a number of other spots people hide spares, nothing is forthcoming. Returning through the window does not prove as easy as rolling in. My bike does not collapse, but does tip over onto the ground leaving me one leg in and one out. A pain from pedaling, or the resurgence of kicking at the vile Jaysie, sends a lightning strike from my ankle up into my groin. If I could get comfortable and just stay where I am I would. The prospect of a move one way or another (Breaking Glass - Blondie, attaches itself to my thought) is punk. To pull back inside I have assessed will be marginally easier and I interpret this as being marginally less painful. But then I will starve and go thirsty. In the morning, I will still need to get out. The door opens outwards, I think this is a Scandi trait. I could just kick the fucking thing to effect my escape. Wincing at the thought of the pain from my already tender leg, I consider the alternative of using chair as a battering ram perhaps. I recollect two or three cans of beans or the like during my search, slightly rusty, lurking, dejected. I take the easy way out. I go back in.

Simplicity it is not. The only thing that works well or at all is the torch. I try to think back to the last time I actually saw anyone here. There is a strong feel of abandonment, desolate in a way far beyond neglect. Painted into a corner and then as the paint begins to peel the rust eats in, like some form of leukaemia, this is even more than I am exposed to – although my skin is the shuck of my exterior while I know my vital organs are being taken by the spirit.

There is a door from behind which emanates a fair whiff. I presume it is a chemical toilet that was not properly emptied. I am reluctant to open it. As I take a few steps, hand reaching out for the handle, my foot then half of my calf disappear through the floor. The whole thing's a rust bucket. I push on down for fear that retraction will see the sharp edges gouging into flesh. It's first attempt has done for my denims. The ground finally takes up my weight. Standing on one exterior leg I use the other to stamp around to make the trap bigger. Strangely the rest of the floor seems to be prepared to fight back and I have to end up jeopardising fingers to bend the claws down and away.

We'd been watching Suits, binge watching on-going seasons, A and me. Fleetingly, I see Donna open a drawer and take out the significant tin opener. Everyone should have a tin opener. The people this place belongs to sure don't. I then understand the long term shun of what I have anticipated would form part, possibly all, of my evening meal. A plastic bottle of cheap cider cheers me up momentarily, until the smell from the previously opened top gives off a distinct smell of pee.

The legs do it, all four squarely on the unglazed bottom section. It is the third assault that I make that takes me and the seat out onto the grass. The chair back nearly cuts me in half as I come crashing down.

For a number of days, I take water from the stream that runs through my foraging patch, it's clear, lacks smell and is reasonably fast running. I remember Bianco drinking here and it did not have ill effects. It taste of nothing. This is another good sign and so it has become my drinking source. I am also picking greenery to provide salad to go with the ham I am eating. The knife I should be using is long and thin for cutting fine slivers, the blade I have is thicker, shorter and cuts off chunks which makes the dried meat chewy and hard to swallow.

I sleep in the van, wash and do my toilet in the stream further on down.

During the day I seem to sleep a lot. When I'm not, I find myself chanting ingredients reminiscent of some sort of mantra.

media cottura

misto

osso buco

marinato

imbottito

granchio

frullato

formaggio

crudo

petto

lauro

budino

coniglio

calamaro

brasato

abbacchio

arrosto

zimino

timo

stracciato

Ten days is a good time period I think, the number of days I have allotted myself to remain off the grid. The time I have given Angela to realise I have gone. The time I assess she will need to realise she misses me and will come looking. She will not find me, of this much I am aware, but when I show up she will have been drained of all the malice she has been harbouring. The Prodigal returns and all that rubbish.

After only eight days, my resilience has slipped away. I am hoping Angela has also reached an earlier feeling of loss than I had originally allowed for. I pack up nothing; the door is beyond locking. I straddle the bike and begin pedaling. The weather has been grim, but today the sky is clear and the temperature is more in keeping with what I imagine to be the seasonal norm. The outcome of this is, of course, that I am soaked with sweat before I have reached the main road. Hardly an image of desire as I cycle up the lane to the cottage.

The Jag and the Defender are parked side by side. The van is not in evidence and Bianco is not pawing the window or barking at the gate. Angela is not rushing out to take me in her arms, forgive all, strip me and drag me off to the shower. I decide to check out the forge for warmth first. A forerunner of what to expect, a bellwether of sorts. There is no fire, no warmth. I dig deep into the heart of it, the embers are dead. Dead for a while. I do not take anything from this, Angela's focus has been elsewhere. The three-figure gardening project will be all consuming.

Through the window I glance into the cottage, why I am not sure as it is my intention to go inside. I am thinking if Angela is not here to welcome me home, which she clearly isn't, I will be here to welcome her home.

I can see my stuff, my personal stuff, clothing and the like. My shawl, a favourite, a lover's gift, a comfort blanket, hanging from one of a mound of black garbage bags piled in the hallway. My chef mentor, Michelin-starred in food and love, my first female induced orgasm, my Po River Valley silk scialle. Tears wash my cheeks. Memory rejects the circumstances of her lingering death-path, I have no handkerchief, I hear her voice, I wipe away the pain and the brine with the back of my hand. Strewn across the sofa is an edge to edge that is not mine, not Angela's either. I recognise it immediately. I am now taking in everything within the viewing spectrum of the small aperture. There's more. Strewn, dropped, flung in casual untidiness. Bitch. Fucking untidy bitch. The door keys are in my hand, that lot's getting bundled up right now. I'm going to fire up the forge - *the Quattro*. My feet are on fire, my hand shaking, and my mind flicking through the future, but not that much in the future. Images in flick-book fashion of the forge stoked. I'm stoked. I stop, relax. Bring my body and my brain to a perfect standstill. It is now I am no stranger to what has happened. The key is not performing, not due to my quaking, but as a result of the lock being changed.

Half an hour has slipped by. If there had been neighbours, the police would already have been here, but there aren't and they're not. The axe for splitting logs has secured my entry and hacked the alarm bell from the wall, which has toppled me from the unsecured ladder I have had to climb. I am shaken up, bruised some, nothing though to prevent me from capitalising on my intention.

Five armfuls of clothes scooped up, socks crammed with the haul of face art shit, now piled as Guy Fawkes on the top, Vesuvius. I am feeling great affection for my blow torch, pleasure flows up my arm. Warmth in both directions. Liquids, smellies in small assorted shaped bottles, twisted to suit, which the bitch can't afford and will not go up in smoke I am pouring over my side the bed, then I degrade Angela's for good measure. I need to go for a dump, then on a whim using one of Bianco's poo bags make a retrieval and smear excrement over the inside of the fridge. This is disgusting and I have surprised myself. But truly, I'm a nice person and I don't deserve to be treated like this. I'm sure I'm not the arse-hole in all this.

Of course, I am pissed and that probably makes a difference, not an excuse, but I say it to remind myself that I did take a big swig from a bottle of spirit as soon as I got in, mainly to kill the pain from the fall. I note also alcohol is again jake. And the second, I am now judging was deeper and longer to ease the psychological hurt of finding evidence of Jaysie in my bed. Epidermal cell turnover, innocent cells surfacing as the dead cells on the surface flake away. 50 million skin cells a day, so lets say at least double that with Angela clawing at her back.

I feel justified (not ancient) as I walk out the door. I leave everything in the black sacks, except the shawl and Bianco's sleeping rug, which I have thrown into the rear of the Defender. I guess I'm not coming back.

It maybe Jaysie's wardrobe will topple while still in flames and incinerate the whole of the studio. It had been a spark in my mind to blowtorch the bed, but Bianco stopped me, or the thought that he would have nowhere to live. That and the fact that the canister emptied before the flame had time to achieve any ignition.

I have driven straight back to the caravan, although straight might have been in time rather than direction. I have recollection of sideswiping, well more slightly grazing I'm sure, a parked something or other, not a skip, some sort of vehicle. But I didn't stop, and I didn't get stopped. Although if I had been, I didn't much care.

o0o

I write things down. It is something I used to do regularly when small in Italy. I have paper, and a Biro which pisses me off as it creates the words by blobbing ink patches at least once on each line. Why this causes me dismay is ridiculous, as I have no illusion that it will be read by anyone else. And if I am honest, once the line is committed to the page I will never bother with it again.

I have reached the third page, six sides, and the spirit is rapidly wearing off. I open and savour, yes I am savouring and appreciating the taste of the first bottle I have opened from the swag I took some nine days ago. This, I conclude, proves I'm not a piss head. The lapse between obtaining it and the appreciation of the flavour – I am enjoying, evaluating, understanding.

I think of other things I did as a kid at home and start to write about these.

Strega comanda color blue was a good colour when I was the witch, which I did enjoy, calling brown or green or white made it too easy. surprisingly few things in blue were reachable and even the tallest kids couldn't touch the sky. I love the Italian blue sky I think I was the only one that enjoyed being strega getting to call the colour sending all my friends scatting to grab that before I could grab them of course as soon as one got caught I became one of the find the colour kids which was a little boring. run run run I cried chasing the fastest. most went after Maria when it was their turn to call and catch she was podgy slow and flat footed and would often hold something of the wrong colour. I'm thinking now as well as having two flat feet she may have been colour blind. Poor thing I can't imagine what has happened to her.

I'm finding writing therapeutic, well I would if I thought I needed therapy. Having nearly finished the bottle I feel hungry. My belly is rumbling, but I decide I am more tired than I am starving. Tomorrow will be less hard work, less stressful. I will forage and start eating fresh food, exercise. Get healthy.

A heavy red is a heavy head. I drink from the open bottle. It is raining during the early morning. I roused chilled so pulled the cork on a lighter vintage, drank half with determination. It burned off the cold and plunged me down into the sleep-coma alcohol has the beauty to conjure up. Awake now and colder than ever, it is not cold out just wet. The damp in my bones is pulling at my skin, it reminds me of hiding in the caves in the hills behind my home. Determined not to be caught. Guardie e Lardi – really was my giochi preferito.

My favourite game I remember now was always cops and robbers.

I have written this down, just the one line in English. I will scribble something about it more later when I have eaten. I know the gas ring has gas but I've no way of knowing how much. I want to use it sparingly but getting warm now must surely not be a waste. I make a hot drink and tip in too much sugar, not more than I intend but too much for normal tastes.

oOo

A threadbare carpet of white has flashed across the ground, I think it is blossom. Conker trees have white flowers. It is a flurry of early snow, but this has not been clear through the grim veiled windows, it is only discovered as I leave for some reason that has slipped my memory. My face is cut by the cold. I return inside. From the floor I pick up a shopping list that is covered with foot prints from various tramplings. Some with shoes, some with toe prints from unencapsulated feet.

Large bags pasta twirls
Large bags rice (cheapest)
Case tomato puree
Chilli flakes
Salt
Strong cider - all that money can buy

I look around and can find no evidence of pasta, rice, or the rest. Except 2 litre bottles of cider everywhere. Most still undrunk. There is no sign of empty bags of food, dirty dishes or used saucepans. I have a fleeting remembrance of discarding everything that wasn't liquid when it came to paying. But it can't be relied upon. I think back and consider the possibility the items listed that remain unfound could still be in the back of the Defender. On further investigation this is proving to be incorrect.

I'm thirsty, so I drink.

o0o

Devils on Horseback is a surrogate for oysters wrapped in bacon, but here there are no angels at any expense. Wrap a dried fruit Ficus carica, a species of the flowering tree of the mulberry species, in streaky dry cured bacon. Most chefs use prunes, but I know where fig trees grow locally wild. Skewer with a cocktail stick and cook till crisp.

I call the order from the pass.

'Ça Marche, un covert, un diables à cheval'

Maria is the Maitre d', flat footed she has arrived demanding, her little voice screaming urgently up.

'Servizio. Servizio'

I am relying on kitchen French – very traditional internationally, she is sticking to her native Italian. Although I know, in France prunes in a shirt is the expression – *pruneaux dans une chemise*

The brigade are all aged eleven and twelve, dressed in white jackets with blue and white dogtooth shorts, their heads protected by pointed British constables helmets. They guard the treasure. Pounding, pounding, pounding. Horses hooves. The Charge of the Light Brigade. A waiter whose face is in shadow continues to clap the coconut shells in gallop rhythm. At the kitchen goods entrance, the stallions of the four horsemen rear up to ride roughshod through. Horse spit from lathered lips and flared nostrils spray like globules of water from a swirling shaggy dog as the beasts spurred on by dinner-suited riders in Lone Ranger masks circle the range and in this commotion the Devils are snatched, flat foot is padding into the safety of the restaurant. The Devils are winning the day.

Was I the judge in collusion? Could I have done more? This was not of my making. I hold no responsibility here. I sit at a white tablecloth and eat my lunch.

Sex toys, some still in their packaging, others in the shower,I am hacking at with the chopper I axed my way into the cottage with. Vibrators in the guise of fungus are in the hands of naked, young children reminding me of the Oz cover 28 School for Kids; podostroma cornu-damae the most poison one is being rammed into the throat of an unwilling young woman, which feels like me. Red and deadly. Dead and red.

The telephone box is where I'm heading. They are all morto. The fat man has the receiver to his ear and someone alongside of me is saying he is calling me. He wants to explain, my vomit still encrusts his clothing, his features have also not been washed. He has credit cards, notes and coins, which are not able to be fed. Vandalised. People are being packed alongside. Five foot, everyone must be five foot for it to count, I hear a dwarf with a clipboard yelling. A man with a small moustache is being dragged away shouting he is not German. They hold the record, it was twelve but now the Scots have it at fourteen.

'I'm Charlie.'

More people squeeze. Jaysie is being pushed up into the space above other participants' heads. Angela is present, tearing down postcards from prostitutes, and a faceless figure with flowers in her hair shoves pizza and hamburgers into her mouth.

Why does he want me. I'm here. I have become invisible, but I am here on the outside. With the fat man around they'll never break the record.

'Push him out. Take me, take me.'

Hammering, banging, they are in here. Dead dog in arms, laying out on the table. Tears.

'Fuck off. Get out.'

Not sure if this is them or me.

I am being beaten with a stick as the physical and verbal onslaught backs me into a corner. Old faces in my face. I am pushing, kicking, rolling, the window falls away and I am scrabbling out, away, feet naked chaffing raw, branches whipping my face, the cold numbing my earlier damaged ankle. I fall, stare down, my leg has a balloon on it's end. Nothing.

Teeth chattering, ice cold, the taste of blood, pitch dark. Hell is hot, flames give light. Inferno this is not. I pray it is not heaven. Dio is not replying. I turn my words to the Devil and am equally ignored.

Again nothing.

My knees are scabbed, my fingernails broken, I want to vomit, my nasal tubes are filled with the most obnoxious fumes, fumes or just smell but enough to retch. I need to puke, I fall my feet unstable on empty cider bottles. I crash into the loo, which I assume to have been my destination.

I yell tormented in terror and stumble away trying to slam the fragile door as I go. The face of the dog, head hanging over the side of the chemical toilet bucket is tattooed onto my vision, tongue protruding skull lolling with the motion of my crazy jive. The fact there is no food in my gut does not prevent contents being located and projectiles of near shit peppering the walls, furniture, and all other contents in a 210 degree radius. The red running down the smooth surfaces looks suspiciously like blood.

I vow never to return.

'Dead dogs giblets green phlegm pie.'

'The horror. The horror. Is this the start of the apocalypse?'

I wake up with the engine running and the heater on. Filling the tank before buying the cider was the best move I have made in longer than… I am biting my tongue. I am shaking, but not from the cold. I manage to roll onto my side before the hot pokers sear my inner organs.

The darkness of heaven or hell takes me.

The images are black and white. Some have subtitles. It is the day of the standing dead. Little Boy and Fat Man. I am staring at the ground, watching it push through. Baby Magpie it is not, as the light gets brighter, redder, my skin is burning. The growing does not stop. It is my writer's birthday, August 5th but like me he has yet to be born. It will take another day to overshadow the world. Big big big, the mushroom will kill all in it's pyrocumulus shadow. Someone hands me a phone. It is the fat man.

'You will never escape the fallout, 101101101'

I wake momentarily, my arms legs and torso are bleeding from nails tearing my skin. I can't live without alcohol. I fall back into a coma with the phrase *cold turkey* in my epileptic brain.

More darkness. The night sky is a possibility. The engine is off. How I'm lucid enough to take note of this baffles me. No diesel. Stalled. Turned off – by who? I can see I have in some fitting state kicked the rear door open, lock broken, hanging. I am pulling the dog blanket, Bianco's rug, around me. And as I slip away I can feel I have bitten through my lips. I do not expect to surface a third time.

The tongue of the horse is slobbering saliva around my cheeks, across my mouth, filling my ears, blinding my eyes and smothering my breathing. The first of the four stallions have returned. My transport awaits. Will there be sandwiches for the trip, I wonder. The smell of the beast is not unrecognisable to me. Corked wine envelops my senses. Cider maybe. I try to pinpoint. Wine, not stale cider of any kind, although the apple alcohol is surely what the greatest argument demands. What is the smell associated with Hell? Brimstone or sulphur or are these the same thing? Regardless is this what I can smell? No, I'm sticking with my original thought. I wipe my nose with the back of my hand, my nostrils clear the smell intensifies. Still no reason to convert. The horse is not smooth haired. My vision is blurred, I rub both eyelids with the back of my hand spreading snot which was not what I intend. I can see less and contemplate ever seeing longhaired horses. My memory recalls a hypoallergenic breed, a wealthy abitante del villaggio imported an American curly coated horse for his allergy-ridden daughter. She said it was a biscuit but I think she had the name wrong.

Looking back I will remember the moment it all came flooding back. I sobbed, I cried, tears ran down my cheeks. I hugged and kissed.

I was lost and now I am found.

How, will forever remain a mystery.

I will speculate.

A friend once had a spaniel, called Dylan if I recall, who during an unsupervised period in the exercise patch, an area with high fencing but without a roof, had scaled the chain-link and escaped the kennels in which he had been incarcerated. Covered in mud, tongue lolling, he made a brief appearance at his home, which was in fact no more. The property he knew had been sold and his owners moved on. Dylan, scheduled to be collected and introduced to his new home in three weeks had not been made aware of this and had taken what he considered the necessary action to reunite with his parents. Realising the change in status, Dylan had hit the road. Sightings were reported in response to 'Lost Dog' posters distributed by the embarrassed kennel operators and the distraught owners of their absent pet. Three months later, when all hope had tapered off and plans were afoot for Dylan 2, Dylan 1 was found paint-stripping the newly coated front door when his owners motored up the drive.

Was this Bianco's story? A daring abscondment and covert flight over days, weeks, longer. A painstaking search, across the Garden of England, each previously visited early morning exploration, located, and meticulously finger-tipped for clues or proof of abandonment.

The beginning and the end of Dylan's journey can be verified but that which links them must remain speculative.

I continue to wonder.

I look into his eyes. People have said they can see a person in there. I can see that person too.

The adrenaline rush, the sparkle at tracking down his quarry, I can see is draining away. The physical vibrance has subsided, the eyes beginning to glaze over. I trace his body with my palms, fingers exploring and receiving an antipathetic snap as I locate the right dew claw which is missing. He knows my intention is well meaning but has wanted to let me be aware of the pain he feels. Gently I part the hair and can see it has been ripped way. The rest of him is without visible damage. Although this does not relate to the matting, the unprotected ribcage. An ounce of fat there is not, what was a powerfully muscular body is no longer displayed.

Bianco is in need of my help, but I am in no position to tend to my own life support. The ham is finished, the bone discarded, collected to feed foxes or other carnivorous wildlife during the hours of darkness. The greenery of a forage will not nourish a dog or return Bianco to health. I have coin but insufficient to buy anything to nutrify either of us. I pour water and he drinks from the torrent, exposing bleeding gums. I do not want to return to the interior of the caravan. A nightmare I have no wish to relive. It holds horrors similar in revulsion to my TV debut. I have recollection of a couple of cans of dog food, one I know was blown which was sufficient when I fleetingly considered them for my own dinner. The fact they were of poor quality and did not display ring-pull lids were additional factors that they remain on the shelf.

With no other option I close down all my senses, dash in and retrieve the two cans. The one not blown is without a label so could easily be spaghetti hoops or mulligatawny soup. I assumed them to be of similar content I guess due to their proximity to each other and identical shape. But are all cans not identical. Without an opener I place the container on a rock and smash it with a stone, several times. Eventually it is hewn. I think of Angela. Meat not resembling anything not mechanically recovered oozes out. I poke about with a stick, bits cling like an almost eaten toffee apple. Bianco is reluctant but with encouragement he eats like a teenager being offered brassicas. I will not entertain the thought of the blown can although now Bianco's juices are invigorated and he is expectant.

I settle him on the rug and wedge the door closed from the outside. He is acceptant.

I need money. I push the wheels twenty yards so the clunking sound does not upset him. Sleeping dogs etc., mount and peddle off in the direction of the road. Begging is an option, stealing another. The state I am in adds to the homeless beggar characterisation. It then dawns on me, I am a homeless beggar. I should have brought Bianco, the inclusion of a dog I have witnessed forms part of a successful performance. As I come onto the tarmac the light is fading, I turn left instead of right. I have not ventured in this direction previously. Two trucks are parked in a lay-by. One is dark, unattended with it's back door open. I have often been curious as to the purpose of this when I have viewed similar while driving around. I have no goods, I am empty. Don't waste your time I guess is the message. So I don't.

In the other a light shines in the cab. The number plate is not English. I cycle by, dismount and walk back to try my luck. The place is deserted, this seems to be the only sponging bet so I realise failure will mean returning empty handed or going on for miles.

He is standing in front of me leaning back against the side of the trailer, short, hairy, in need of a bath and carrying a gut. His trousers and pants are around his knees and I am crouched in front of a limp thing, which I have never found attractive. In his hand he is holding three ten-pound notes which represents the agreed money I will earn for the blow job. I had knocked on the window, standing on the footplate with my nose pressed against the glass. It is not a Lexus and he is not a high roller. I have rubbed my finger and thumb together and pointed to my mouth indicating my hunger and the need to buy food. He gives me an international hand gesture for fucking but which I believe is of Italian origin. He is Eastern European. We bargain over gift or wages. I finally capitulate but refuse the interior of the cab.

I throw my head back, run my fingers through my hair and as my hand falls I snatch the notes and spring from my mental starting blocks. Abuse in a tongue unfamiliar follows, gaining in volume by the moment. I glance over my shoulder, which I should know will slow me down but not as fast as the leg cuffs of my pursuer. My ankle is playing up but I am already on the bone-shaker and legs turning before my disappointed john has his pants above his thighs. His first few steps have sent me back to school. Sports day, sports teacher demonstrating the finer techniques of the sack race. I was eight.

The remainder of my pay I had stuffed in my pocket at the outset. Half a kebab. I should but I don't know if these make edible dog food but it is the best I can do. Back at the Defender, I drink flat cider and tempt Bianco with cold pitta and fatty lamb which I have meticulously washed free of lashings of chilli.

First thing, I will drive to the village to buy food for Bianco and see if I can lay my hands on more cash to pay for a vet to look him over.

A pink tongue is licking my face, the rear door is open and the sun is high past midday. Two 2 litre bottles, empty of cider are topless next to me. I have been in such a deep sleep I have not heard Bianco get the door open and jump down for his call of nature. Sleep. Don't lie. Drunk. Again. That's the honesty of it. Bianco came through thick and thin to find his master and what he found was a drunken, homeless, street hustler.

I vow to be the person he is entitled to.

I wash, head to foot in water that should be in block form it is so cold. I dry using the dog rug and then rub my body with leaves I pick that smell I think of hyacinth. I dress and my body odour returns virtually unmasked. My clothes need washing more than I did, but they will not dry.

The woman in the convenience store does not take her eye off me. I don't think she recognises me but is worried for her stock. I have a list in my head.

Baby socks.
Trays of chicken breasts.
Eggs
Matches
Scissors and comb
Dish wash liquid
Lighter fuel
Dog mixer
No alcohol

I have to buy a fucking bag. But as I hoped I have change in my pocket. I drive back to the caravan. Bianco is half asleep on the journey quietly whimpering. The smell as I open the Defender door has the waft of an undiscovered murder scene. The wind must have changed direction. I can't be here, not sober at any rate.

Everything that's around worth keeping, which is next to nothing, I load into the vehicle. I create a mask from large dock leaves and go inside the place I have camped out in for weeks on end. I stand the Calor gas container on the ring, turn it on and strike a match. The blue container will blow itself to pieces and everything around. I squirt the other areas with the lighter fuel holding enough back for the purpose it was purchased for - setting fire to wet wood. I flick a match to each and the flames take hold and begin to spread. I leave.

I return. I dash back in against my better judgement and scrap up all the notes I have written which are strewn across the table. Then I'm gone.

I have no destination. No additional funds, no plan to execute.

I am tempted to go to the Baby Magpie birthplace to face my demons but the temptation is not great and easily given a wide birth.

In a distant hollow the explosion comes like a far off bellow of thunder. I wonder if anyone else is close enough to be distracted and inquisitive sufficiently to track down the cause. Maybe. So what.

I drive over a bridge over the motorway, see various woods but those suitable have had their entrances blocked by rubble put there by landowners to prevent gypsies or I suppose people like me taking up residence. I think back to the plume of smoke. I believe what I have done is of gypsy ritual. Does this mean anything I ponder and then abandon. Eventually after going around country lanes, round in circles, crossing previously crossed cross roads I see a gap in the hedgerow that I have driven past before without it attracting my attention. I turn in.

Stopped, I pull the hedgerow back into shape and kick leaves making an effort to cover my tracks. Deeper in, I find what might have been a clearing but now has heavy ground cover and is sheltered from the clouds by an umbrella of tightly knit branches.

I set up camp.

Over a fire, I cook two chicken breasts. One each. Bianco's, I chop finely. Raw is his preference, but I believe cooked will be easier to digest. He looks seriously unwell. I feed him a little at a time and pour him small amounts of water. Big dogs are prone to twisted gut, I know this, in his half-starved state his stomach could easily shrink then twist and bloat. Easy.

In the night I cook again, and feed a little more. In the morning I make us both scrambled eggs. I would like to be using a medicated shampoo, but the funds needed to last. I warm water, wash him and trim away the matted hair. He is not happy but seems too weak to cause trouble. I have finished him and now I do the same for myself using a wing mirror. It is the first time I have seen myself in months or been aware it has been my own reflection I have caught sight of, I reflect. And on reflection calculate my appearance puts me close or below the state at which I have assessed Bianco.

I need a plan. We'll both end up as skeleton-heads if I don't make something happen. Dog walker finds dog and walker. It's a headline. It's a headline that sparks a memory I have filed without first reading. I attempt to place where I picked it up. Maybe it is purely an illusion.

DE REGIO REOPENS
WITH APPOINTMENT OF NEW CHEF

I visualise Jaysie pictured underneath. Surely if it were true, the minute I laid eyes on it I would have sky-rocketed. If it is real, the only place the circumstance would suggest would be during my episode with the blow job.

I put it to one side, and concentrate on the other part of my recollection. I can do this. It's a real shit thing, but if my future and Bianco's is to become more than another filed intention ... Our camp will not be a for-long home. The smoke of the fire, the smell of food cooking or the true walker and dog will bring down the displeasure of the landowner, farmer, gamekeeper or someone representing the legal system.

I cycle out. And in daylight, search likely pitches. A week later, plying my trade has netted four paydays. I am walking Bianco and his strength is building. This and my nightly runs is seeing us both less than gym fit, but a few steps further away from death's door.

My heart is pounding, blood pumping, feet grasping for traction, mud sliding, ears setting out the abuse in foghorn Scouse. Closing, closing, closing. I grab my bike but have no time to mount. The mouthy bastard's a triathlete, naked from the waist with no shame, meat and two veg bouncing in all directions. The cycle I have thrown in his path is being vaulted without a blink. His right toe kicks away my left heel. Down. Bootless foot stuck in, breath taken, vision clogged, dragged up by the scruff, knocked down by clenched fist. I'm pulled without attention to the surfaces I'm being exposed to, I'm dropped as I struggle, knelt over

'Where's the stash lover?' he growls with a menace I can no longer escape.

Hardly open, from the rear door of the Defender, the navvy truck driver breeder's thick fingers around the handle is crashing backwards, his clasp is insufficient to maintain his balance.

I've never seen, not that I can actually see. More imagination. True or false. Bianco has kept me dry. Nothing since he found me. I've never seen behaviour like this. The badly cut white fur is all over him. No barking. Little growling. Bianco's head rises, blood like the rabbit's or hare gives a smudged lipstick look. Both arms are up, crossed, building protection. Head down, Bianco is feasting.

Minutes in slo-mo. Five, ten, an hour it's not. I call him off. I stamp on the ankle but am not heavy enough to cause damage. I repeat the attack with a log. My protector is standing back four square, watching my hammered blow. I am standing. I look down at the half naked dog food, lumps have been bitten from the brachii, the shoulder, cheek and the left, no the right ear has been devoured. Unconscious, but alive. No blood pumping.

If I leave him where he lies he might never be found. Packing up camp is nothing. Bianco, fed and coming down, licks his mouth clean. In less time than Bianco's deliverance lasted, and my pain aside, I have the Defender turned pointing out. I have the part eaten breeder roughly tied by his ankles to the back chassis. I don't want traces of blood in the vehicle. Slowly, even gently I ease our way out trawling over the path I had been dragged down, to return the favour but not looking to add injury to insult. I leave twenty pounds in his wallet and pocket the rest. The credit cards are tempting but common sense tells me no. He is wearing a Rolex, which I take but can't imagine it is not a fake.

CHAPTER SEVEN

I am driving north, heading for the M26.

I am outside Bristol at a petrol station rinsing Bianco with free water, it's cold and he thinks it's miserable of me. Ten minutes have passed and I am buying a bag, toiletries, Tampax, although I haven't had a period for months, longer, probably from when the drinking took hold, and clothes in a supermarket. I am moving on. I ask directions to a public swimming pool and am directed to Bristol South. Standing in the shower, I can't remember when I previously felt this good.

In a library I go on-line and find a kennels not too far away. I address an envelope, sign a cheque and pop it in the post.

At the kennels, I take Bianco in, pay the maid and she encourages him with difficulty to leave. He thinks bad of me I know. I tell him it's for his own good. I leave.

I have cleaned the inside of the Defender myself, now like a swarm of flies a team of Eastern Europeans are all over it with sprays and chamois. Back in the supermarket I eat and by a burner and load it up – the world is my oyster.

It is suddenly my intention to catch the train into London, but the Embassy tells me they can't do anything under thirty days. The cottage is now like a magnet, drawing me closer to all the shit that has happened to me over the past months, which with Bianco's help I thought I'd left behind.

I still don't want to go and now three hours later parking a short walk across the field I'm here and I know I will. If I go in, which I will, I chance being demonically possessed. Walking out will not shed the contagion that may infect me. I laugh at myself, this is some Catholic fear culture. But now I'm remembering the Italian courts granting a man a divorce only months ago because he claimed his wife was possessed.

Where is my saviour when I need him? I have sent him away, for his own good. This is a battle I must fight alone. I am fit now and I have a plan that necessitates me being here.

I establish the cottage is empty and hope the locks have not been changed a second time. I use the keys, no change, the alarm sounds, I am at the number pad keying in the code. All remains active. I wonder if Angela has had it linked to the police station or to the security firm. Or will it just annoy the distant neighbours. I lock up and leave. It takes half an hour for a police car to arrive. No armed response. A disinterested shake on the door, a casual walk around the building with the occasional glance through the windows. I wait thirty minutes and set it off again. It takes an hour before the engineers arrive and another hour before they have finished checking the system over. My knees and back are killing me. I feel like Houdini, I rack my brain while huddled in a corner of the studio that is my hide and do not remember his real name. It will come to me.

I am ready to set it off again when Angela turns up. I hate her. She looks great. I am keeping my fingers crossed; if she comes into the studio it will not take more than a few minutes for me to be unearthed. I wonder what I will do if it happens, how I will react. How she will react. There is one upside. It's not Jaysie. The lights go on, the curtains are closed. I take the opportunity, fight or flight. I'm away.

This is not good.

It's three in the morning and I find myself once again asleep in the Defender. I'm cold and in need. If I had some booze to hand I'm sure I'd be necking it.

Three days have passed and only now has a second kick at the can presented itself. I have moved each night so as not to raise the attention returning when the possibility of the cottage being empty is at it's highest. I can guess when Jaysie will be at work, so have steered clear till then.

All looks quiet. I telephone and no one picks up. I am there, keys in hand, sweaty, in the lock, door open. The ring begins. I am giving myself fifteen minutes and on past performance that should give me at least fifteen minutes margin for error. Or unluckily, the police are on a shout that's over close by.

I'm focused. I know what I want and I know where it should be. It is and I pocket it. On a whim I go to the kitchen, open the fridge and take a peek. Nice. Good stuff. But I suppose I should expect no less. I take the lid off what could be two portions of osso bucco and spit in it. I smile and replace the lid. Then I find I'm doing something really stupid. But I do it anyway. I see Jaysie's diary and snatch it up, a trophy that will alert them to the intrusion. The one thing I wanted to avoid. But the spitting and the stealing I am telling myself are both control mechanisms. The exorcisms of the demons. It's me not them that has the power. Wonder woman, I fly.

o0o

Dark clouds, green rolling seas. Green faces with rolling eyes. Gaunt, vomiting faces. Hands across mouths as if this will in some way stop beer and fast food from becoming shards of projectiles, scatter gun wars between teams of fellow travellers. The journey is ferrying me away from what I can't face and other people can't accept. This is my Thimithi, my trial by fire, the thought of dashing across burning embers hot enough to cook black and blue steak seemed far more petrifying than plunging my hand into boiling sugar syrup. My party piece. But this is what this is for me. A final test. Once upon a time it was the smell. Now simply the sight of it is enough. I hold it back. I go on deck. The cold, the wind in my face with salt spray. I lick my lips, it tastes like tears. I stretch out on a bench and think of Bianco. I hope he's alright.

PART THREE

A perilous climb down

CHAPTER EIGHT

Marine birds, the smallest first, followed by the pigeon-sized break cover from the spray-wet cliff-face sea-bound; gulls, the common, the herring and rare ring-billed scatter for the sanctuary of the crystal blue lapping Mediterranean water. Both movement and sound have disturbed them from their camouflaged nests but on this dawn it is not meat nor poultry, nor even fish that is the purpose of the early morning forage. Over-head large birds, which may be geese cruise, on what appears to be a predetermined flight plan unaware of the minor perturbation seven thousand feet below.

Erminia is of course not the cause of alarm, she is thirty to forty metres back having travelled lightly, but now stopped and off the toe-path on the opposite side to the shore line. She calls quickly, knowing Bianco will plunge in after the flapping of wings and squawking dissonance without a second thought, if not reined-in by a stiff command. But these days she is less stern, it is a call of habit rather than desperation. Even the early morning sun here is more than warm. But it would not be the first time she has strained her eyes, shielded the glare in the onset of panic before picking his bobbing head from amongst the white horses. Although she has never yet been called upon to launch the rib.

Erminia has been home now for seven months, maybe a little longer. Although home might be construed as with her family, where she grew up, but that is not the case. Now she thinks casa; Italy. Life is very much as it was in England, well in some respects. In others it is worlds apart. She cooks, she is creating wonderful tasting food. In the town, online, over the phone she is asked *'Where is your restaurant?'* She tells people, 'It is on the beach.'

Asked if they can book a table, she apologises explaining this is not possible. They nod knowingly, of course chefs who cook with such fine ingredients, must be booked many months in advance. She smiles.

Erminia spends much of her time looking back as she does planning the future. Planning implies goals; goals seek successes and set up failings. Stress, stress and more stress. The food she creates now is simple in its complexity, cucina povera. Taste is everything. Towers have toppled, smears, tuiles and dots have been rejected. People come to eat, to enjoy. No pomp, no cerimonia. Critics and the epicurean glitterati have come-by but on those days Erminia has only prepared a dish for four and the quartet of chairs are already filled. Cutting does not curry favour.

Portsmouth to Dieppe via Bristol had been Ermina's escape route of choice, fearing the port of

Dover being much closer may well have been on alert for a young woman travelling with a rabid canine.

She had the appearance of reasonable grooming, not a homeless pariah. People boarding ferries did not dress for dinner. Bianco, although crazy with excitement on first being bailed, laid relaxed snoring in the back of the Defender endowed with piece of mind that had eluded him on the days previous.

Almost to Erminia's annoyance on preparing to board and at disembarkation she was waved through without consideration. The passport she had so felt essential to their escape received not even a cursory glance. Had this been something she had understood she would not have required herself to be packed down Erik Weis style. And there she has it, as she knew she would, winkled out from the back of her brain without a conscious thought.

Today she will only cook lunch and tomorrow probably neither pranzo or cena. Distant nimbus clouds slowly travelling from northern Africa support the prediction she had been given yesterday in the town, of rain later in the week.

At weekends, a young lad scours the cliff paths collecting wood for her and when there is insufficient she will take him in the rib to adjoining bays. From the beginning she was astounded the amount of fuel necessary to keep a good fire for cooking at the right temperature, and a smaller fire pit at the entrance of her living arrangement during the cooler winter nights. Although for the last weeks, this indulgence has not been vital, so she has not made the effort.

Now she will lay the logs in the sand, set the fire using a magnifying glass, and over the coming couple of hours will ensure the embers provide a medium heat. From a bucket she snatches the live snaking eels and chops them into sections, skin-on to provide protection from the heat. The bucket drained of water now accepts the slugs of deep-yellow cold-pressed, encouraging out the powerfully spicy flavours of the Pugliese olive oil, vinegar, and sliced red chilli. While the meaty flesh marinates, Erminia climbs the rough track fifty feet up the cliff-face to the cave where she lives, and the adjoining deep cavity in the rock which, deep back, far from the sunlight and heat of the day is where her produce is lovingly stored. A tray of orecchiette made only with semolina and water will be the pasta shells she will serve with the anguilla.

A crude trolley on small wheels acts as the dumb waiter to transport the ingredients. She slowly feeds the rope through her hands, not allowing it to take pace from the weight of the load. At the shore, she runs up ten small ensigns each the size of a handkerchief. From across the bay, those interested in such will now know diners are restricted to ten. This being the number of portions the eels will feed.

Little stones and a few larger pieces of the cliff, olive and plus-size rustle down from above. Bianco has been off chasing and is now returning, paw pads gripping tightly on a surface no diner would attempt. The last few feet surfing onto the beach and bounding straight for the waves. The sun is getting hotter.

Erminia parted with the Defender in Milan for a large wad of Euros, picked up a one way rental to complete the journey to the south. Where she intended to build a life there would be no need for a car, instead a good price was negotiated on the rib with a reliable outboard. With this, the two powered along the coast investigating the abundance of coves until the one that fulfilled her ambitions had been located. It took another month to set up all she needed to maintain an existence.

Three months in, a visit from the nearest mayor on this unauthorised arrangement was settled on a handshake – lunch for two once a month – a man of honour. Not unheard of, Erminia cited Carlo Levi's book, *Christ Stopped at Eboli*, a graphic account of the poverty of cave dwellers in 1935 and the recent boutique hotel and restaurant opening in a few of the now glamourised caves of Sassi. Not that this is a bandwagon she is seeking to emulate.

A single long table, laid-up in the shade of dry conifer branches brought in from the La Sila forest will seat the first ten to arrive. Over the fire, three sea-soaked spits with sage, bay and eel are turned at intervals over the thirty-minute cooking time, and regularly basted with the marinade using a traditional brush of parsley leaves. The wet wood choking off the burn-through of the spit, while the eel draws on the salt. Cooked, the charred skin will be removed without molesting the flesh. Served with pasta, coastal greens and caraffe of local vino bianco that once would have been shipped in bulk to the famous vineyards of France to blend and support poor harvests there – but is now held in esteem, aged and bottled with labels of the municipality that are gaining credence. Fresh and spicy Incanestrato, DOP sheep's milk Vastedda della Valle del Belice of Sicily and the mixed sheep and goat's milk Basilicata Canestrato fill the cheeseboard. And a selection of fruit, freshly picked to enjoy with the espresso of Sulawesi Toraja, high grown strictly hard bean Guatemalan, with a Brasil Cerrado base. Blends, Erminia changes each week.

When she decides not to cook, Erminia will swim and play a form of water polo with Bianco, which he seems to have taken to and perfected in one way or another. Other times they will take the rib around the coast, beach and climb to a forest to walk, sometimes so far it is overnight.

Each day special in it regularity, until *the* special day she has been anticipating for well over half a year. The sentence. The guilty verdict had been found twenty-three days before, but due to the not-guilty plea, no remorse and a continued insistence of innocence, the judge had held off sentencing while background reports were obtained.

The special day had arrived. Regardless of climatic conditions, this was never going to be a day on the beach. In town, Erminia would frequent an internet caffe and search out the news. Each week Erminia had checked, discarding the news headlines, the economy, the constant swipes at the NHS, with people dying untreated, in long A&E queues, bed-blocking and the rest, the inevitable calculations on the price of property.

Six years. Six fucking years. Cazzo!

Does she deserve it. Does Erminia feel a trace of guilt. Yes and no. In that order.

Now she is not happy, simply in a state of equilibrium. She adjusts her feelings, yes she is happy, ecstatic. She had felt like killing her, just stabbing both of them. Had she settled on that course of revenge she understood, she would not so easily have escaped.

Bianco had saved her again. She could not sentence him to a life of near starvation on the loose or being put down by lethal injection. Inflicting multiple knife wounds was more a conjured up fantasy during an alcohol binge, after all she had already taken the cheque and razored out the stub so it's loss would not be noticed without an investigators eye.

The court case was only reported by results. Details of the defence were not available to her. She mused over how the barrister might have argued the case. The prosecution would have had no difficulty establishing the signature was a forgery. But they would not have looked for a third party hand. Was it penned by the account holder, no. Had the funds been paid into the Accused's account, yes. Open and shut. Case rested.

'I never check my account. There's never enough in there to worry about.'

Not convincing and clearly insufficient to sway a jury.

The term was not harsh, a person in a trusted position embezzling from an employer could expect to go down for as much as ten.

oOo

It was her's, De Regio was her child and il bar her baby. Each week Erminia checked. Back to scan the websites of all the specialist transfer agents. And today it is there.

Leasehold corner site with carpark, A3 catering establishment. Not trading. Nil premium. Maybe suitable for alternative uses subject to the necessary consents including conversion to residential. Freehold also available.

In the picture all the signage has been removed and the windows whitewashed. She will continue keeping an eye also on the residential estate agencies but as of yet nothing.

It takes a further three weeks for the cottage with artist's studio to be listed for sale. Erminia places a call to the agent and enquires if the owner of the property may consider letting it. She is not interested in renting, but is seeking further information.

'I can try asking the client, but she is a little difficult to contact. She placed the cottage on the market and has moved to New York. I can send her an email. If you'd like to give me your details I can get back to you as soon as I hear from her but I wouldn't be too optimistic, I got the impression it was a permanent move. I don't think she is looking at coming back.'

The voice is helpful but, not seeing a sale looming, does not sound put out when Erminia says it's ok and not to bother.

Angela does not use social media, this Erminia is aware of, unless she ponders this has also evolved. But the likelihood is a concentrated search around a New York base will expose her. She will not have evaded someones group selfie. An hour has passed with no luck, Erminia will return and continue later or on the next visit, Bianco has been patient for more than can be reasonably expected.

Outside the caffe, he has made friends, she need not have been concerned. A couple, Swedish Erminia thinks, has understood the power of music sheet bread, a Sicilian melba toast, which Bianco will crunch until the goats come home.

'Ah you are the girl with the dog whose restaurant our friends told us to find,' they say in poor Italian, but a second attempt in English proves understandable. A smile crosses their faces as they put two and two together.

'Today I am not cooking, but in the morning look out for the flags across the bay and get a water taxi. No bookings, just first come first served.'

Their clear fondness for Bianco is the grounds for her *invitation* which on other occasions may well have been a rebuttal. That, and the pleasure in her heart currently of visualising Jaysie sweating in a brigade of kitchen staff feeding volume at £2 an inmate. A figure she seems to recall in one of the tabloids as being the same as the provision for an NHS in-patient. Slops.

'There will be three of us.' The woman speaking nods her head towards a younger woman standing staring into a shop window a few doors down.

Erminia is not sure the *no bookings* has been understood but decides not to labour the point. Her attention has been purchased by the reflection the angle of sun has turned the window into a black mirror providing a distinctive stare back in her direction. A sister, perhaps? The couple sitting and still treating Bianco are too young for it to be a daughter. Is the likeness smiling at her, can she see Erminia's interest or has she picked an artefact the other side of the glass that has brought the warmth to her look?

The young woman forsakes her position and joins the group. They could be identical twins but more youthful. All three are both tanned and blonde, so blonde it is stereotypical. Scandinavian. The blue eyes

Erminia is looking into are so pale one might wonder if they provided sight at all, but they clearly did.

'You should visit Denmark, we have some great restaurants now, the produce is amazing and the chefs outstanding.'

Erminia senses this is offered almost as an invitation. She wants to look away but the eyes will not release her.

'I'd like that,' she answers in a rather stupid fashion, reading something that has not been written.

It is only with the sheet music finished and Bianco bouncing off that the spell is broken and the group break up.

Another month has slipped by, by the time a picture of Angela has been tagged and flashes grinning up onto Erminia's screen. A group of women, alcohol blotched complexions, touting lipstick smeared shot glasses in a Mexican canteena. Angela is not camera facing, her head is turned in profile attempting to kiss the woman's cheek she is joined at the hip to. Clare *Blooming-Dale*, impervious, appears to be cow eyed over the waitress offering up a second bottle of George Clooney's Casamigos Tequila. It is not the liquor Erminia suspects that has piqued her interest.

'You won't hold on to her either,' she muses.

o0o

The first summer of Erminia's and Bianco's new life is drawing to an end. Both think the move has been good, bene. Bianco has improved his understanding of the language and does not prickle now when the town's people call out to him from across the street when they are shopping. Both have become minor local celebrities although he understands his mistress seeks to avoid such adulation. He himself is less ill-disposed.

Papers have recently been obtained providing some vague right to settle there which may or may not prove enforceable if questioned in future by authorities beyond the regional boundaries, or if there is a reform in local politics. In the early days, the only construction work had been the fitting of two solid wood doors of monastery weight, one on the living cavern and the other where the stores are held. Both set back into the recesses so were not readily visible from the beach below. A small bank of solar panels has been purchased and installed which is providing light and will, when bought, run a small refrigeration chest.

Today, a no cooking day, has been earmarked to clear the few possessions they have into the store where for the coming week there will also be a makeshift bedroom – in preparation for a costruttore artigianale to deal with damp areas and render the rough limestone that may be considered unsafe. Erminia has taken the decision to whitewash and decorate it herself. Nothing chic in style, traditionally coastal, and definitely no designs that could be considered Angelaeque.

Sitting at the waters edge, enjoying a glass of wine which she now feels comfortable doing, there are no sorrows to drown, no demons hiding in the darkness. In their place, a strength of character, a confidence she has never before experienced.

It is pleasant, she is relaxed, she reads, and she becomes thoughtful, speculating on herself many years into the future. Will she become the old woman of the short story she is reading; Under Fire is not without its resonance, the foraging, the cooking over open flames, the cliff face. She imagines the forgetfulness of old age and dementia come to all in time. The son is not a likely aspect for her she deliberates, although the firewood boy could be a surrogate. She does not know how she feels at the thought.

In her hand Erminia rotates a business card evidencing a name and a Danish address. She woolgathers thoughts of February in the cold of the north. Then she stretches out her arm and pulls a bag she has never opened in Italy, stuffed with unknown things she must have considered important as they made their flight across the Channel.

The creased and screwed shawl, which she had assumed was lost and gone from her life forever, had prevented the remaining contents from tipping out. The joy a single garment could arouse was unthinkable, but it evokes emotions that other people might find in hearing pieces of music; raising the hairs on the back of her neck and oca bumps along the arms. All this, yes. She smiles and ruffles the coat on Bianco's head.

In the bottom there is just paper. It dawns on her the moments of stupidity, running back into the caravan, flames belching in the swirling drafts, licking at her arms and face as she snatched up the doodlings scratched during the aeons she languished in her piss artist period. Now seeing each sheet, torn, screwed, singed, some with words or images so dense on the page they are undecipherable, other notes on thoughts, which made little sense then, and less now. Some were also blank. One catches her eye. It is written not in her hand but appearing to be both with the use of her pen and paper. She stares at it for more than a long moment without picking it up. Contemplating. Attempting to place it. It is facing the opposite direction, reading it upside down is not making sense. Picking it up she reasons with herself *'I wonder who the letter is from? – Open it stupid.'*

Erminia leans across and lifts the note and corrects its inverted position. She reads the words that look as though they could have been penned while travelling on a train, running on a bumpy track. This can't be the case. She settles on age, old age, a tremoring grasp in boney fingers. Once she has read and understood the message she will add to her thought, emotion and heartbreak.

Paddy is dead We are glad he died before us it worried us to die first This was his favourite place and we know we promised him he would be buried here The van is not ours the people that owned it when they moved on said we could use it now you can use it We are sorry it is in such a bad state but it's been 20 yrs The ground is to hard I tried to dig and Eric tried but he is more frail than me Please dig him a grave when spring comes and the earth softens Maybe you will want to leave him outside until then this is alright the cold will keep him preserved and his soul will not be inside. You will find him in the toilet

We know it is a lot to ask but we will be ever grateful
A & E

The dog in the bog.

It had not been Erminia's intention to cremate Paddy. Torching the van had been an act of destruction, destroying all that remained of a past life. Her past life. She understood the gypsy tradition. It freed the spirit. A cleansing. But what is in someone's brain hiding a dead anything in the loo. She visualises Bianco's inert body in that position and then hates herself for the thought.

'Don't worry I won't do that to you,' she assures him.

He lifts his head and lets it drop back down again. Nothing of interest there. She looks at the signature again. The whole thing is reminiscent of the ongoing news from the UK, reports of bodies being left on trollies in corridors.

It is not until moving back into her cave a few days later – bright, white and reflective – that she now has cause to move the bag of memories and revelations again. Why or possibly how she did not pull it out after the shawl, or the screwed notes, is not clear to her – apart from the thought she recalls it was her understanding the bag was empty. But as she hooked it high on a peg in a line of short sticks she had hammered into a crevice to provide additional hanging facilities for the few belongings she owned along with Bianco's lead, rarely worn, and other dog paraphernalia, it tipped out from the base where it had firmly fitted itself. The hard backed book, square and the same colour as the lining, was an easy thing to have overlooked in the confessions of the previously discovered contents. Erminia christens this bag the bag of stupidity. How stupid it had been to take the book, a dead giveaway, proof somebody had been in the cottage. If caught, proof she had been in the cottage.

Bringing through the remainder of her kit had now to wait, any repercussions of possession had long since faded. The spoils of war were now free to be enjoyed. Despite each page being ultra fine, the book was thicker than she remembered and heavier than it had felt when snatched up. The writing varied, neat – probably written while sitting at a table or desk; scribbled – maybe notes made while pressing on a soft surface, sitting in bed came to mind; jumpy with points in incorrect places for the normal shape of a letter penned either in English or Italian. A multitude of instruments with an equal number of refills of varied colours, all of which appeared to have no relevance on the subject being recorded.

The first entry made following Jaysie's application for the position of sous at De Regio, the second thoughts prior to interview and the third jumpy on the journey home after interrogatorio.

'Is that what she thought my asking her to cook was,' Erminia speaks out loud, half laughing and partially huffing a note of caustic contempt.

Looking back it was a well-mastered performance both in execution and presentation.

Some of the sexier entries were thoughts written in Italian and some of these avoided comprehension or translation as some form of cypher had been invented to keep her deepest feeling or perhaps ratings of conquests, liaisons or in actuality the greater volume simply fantasies.

Certainly there were no truths or fabrications that could be gleaned in erotic narrative gesturing towards either herself or Angela. Was it that, that she was hoping to have exposed, some Freudian rationale to her behaviour. Conceivably, greed and ego were the only drivers.

Not long back Erminia had spent many months on the margin of life, and it is at this moment the margins give up the clues, if not the spelled out answers, to matter that were of deep concern buried sufficiently far below to no longer interfere with the life once not even imagined, but now basked in.

Destroying Angel: These words had been noted in the side and later Erminia presumes as different inks have been used, crossed through, with the comment '*2 much*'.

Erminia knows of this from her many hours researching the Baby Magpie discovery and before that, the general mushroom fact finding investigations. She understood why Jaysie would be attracted to the name. But she recalls, it is a killer with no means of cure, destroying liver and kidneys and all sorts of horrible stuff.

A second mushroom name had been written and this had remained. No pencilling through this one – *Ivory Funnel.* Erminia knew this one even by it's Latin name, it had remained in her memory courtesy of a comment made by Angela while looking over her shoulder and urging her 'get naked' instead of being a boring bookworm. The *Clitoybe blanchi. Vomiting and diarrhoea, but not deadly.* Also known as the sweating mushroom.

'If it's sweating you want, I'll do that for you.'

Erminia had given up and allowed herself to be lured into bed.

Pushing away what she and Angela had shared together, all was beginning to clip into some kind of pattern. She felt she should be surrounded by all involved, her Agatha Christie or Death in Paradise moment. Instead it was for the benefit of herself and Bianco. Neither perpetrators, just victims. But victims with retribution, in which she takes some comfort.

Between notes, comments and ingredient adjustments that Jaysie believed would improve and turn what she considered Erminia's not quite perfect recipes into her own accomplished dishes were thoughts on how she would depose her boss and step into her shoes.

It seemed transparent to Erminia that moving on, finding a sponsor and opening her own place was not sufficient, she wanted to be her. De Regio, il bar, Angela, move into the cottage and the foraging. Surprisingly the number of times Bianco was mentioned in a negative mien indicated he was the only aspect to be axed.

'Well how could anyone not think you are just the best Bianco,' Erminia said, providing a reassuring smooth. 'Well probably not bollock naked truck drivers,' she added appreciatively.

Erminia continues to flick through the pages and then she finds it. What she knows will be there and there it is.

FUCKING MUSTARD!

Entered and dated the night of the Professional Grande Saucier event.

Better than I could have hoped for in my wildest dreams

Later Erminia will read what has been written following that, but first, right now she needs to hear how her downfall was orchestrated.

Tried to follow E, took bike but gone when got there really bloody early thought to hang around to see time gets back and work out distance doesn't work don't know how long she stays Not straight there and back…

No way to find what she has found have offered to go with her but she so fucking secretive…

Need to think of new plan…

E applied and accepted for PGS event has asked me to be her commis fucking face on it I agreed now ave to come up with idea to make shit of it all…

Have decided to change her silly mushrooms that don't taste special anyway for some that are horrible…

It is here the notes of the two types of fungus have been written in the margin.

This one sounds perfect even better get the judges to puke…

Where to find ivory funnel…

Uncultivated grassland, roadside verges and in sand dunes monday will go to camber…

Checked on line seems to have little taste perfect and a slight sweet smell no problem..

Camber waste of time…

Back to thetford forest time getting short…

Will try freezing if no good will need to go back just before show on line says finished in december maybe dry some…

Fuck fuck fuck I hate thetford spent hours and found none…
Went to kingswood could have picked bags not 2 far slipped in the mud…

Erminia puts the journal down and pours herself a glass of wine. Jaysie's muddy boots do not escape her recall. How could she have been so moronic asking Jaysie to be her assistant, she agonises at the idea the girl could be anything but toxic.

She contemplates sending it to the police, the police in England. *Did Angela know?* – is another thought that comes to mind. This is sounding ridiculous to her but finding it had not taken a great deal of searching, it was almost just laying around. She had seen it, picked it up and taken it on a whim. Sipping the cold 2014 Statti Mantonico Bianco, she is looking to accompany a Zuppa di Pesce, evaluating the compatibility of the almond and fig flavours in the finish of this white bottled locally from grapes planted by the Greeks and offering the consistency more of a red wine. It is wonderful, but her focus is elsewhere.

She returns to reading, still only selecting the lines relating to Jaysie's covetous deed. Her childish remarks are simplistic and boring.

Need to fix on a way for the judges to be affected everything says half hour before feeling the effect this sounds difficult by the time it starts working the whole show could be over and E might have won not that she's capable then how to get them to eat enough for it to work in some cooking shows the judges seem to take less than a bite before moving on…

Have thought about it but have not worked it out yet…

Not the judges it must be E she… she… what… what must she…

Twenty minutes to half hour two mushrooms at least decided to make small dish and get her to eat before show gets started make her understand its important to keep her blood sugars up when everything starts stressing and then keep feeding tasters right up to service…

'And I swallowed it whole,' Erminia tells Bianco.

Bianco growls softly, his look she assesses is one of condemnation.

'You are right of course,' she tells him, understanding the censure he is tendering.

She feels her mind is beginning to match the clearness of the liquid she is appreciating more with each taste. Any thought of sending an anonymous package of evidence to the police she now discards and the shadow idea of posting it or a copy of it to Angela is also trashed.

The following day she is peeling away the onion-skin pages individually and adding them to the flames of the lunchtime fire. The cover is too thick and she feels it may take longer to burn and degrade the quality of the embers which will impart their smokiness to the cinnamon-rubbed roasted goat meat she will serve as a deconstructed capretto, the onion, aubergine and passata forming the sauce for the ruote pasta. When all is eaten and her guests ferried back across the bay – the cover, the last true reminder of the part of her past she is determined to erase will be incinerated in the dying embers.

THE END

UNDER FIRE

A SHORT STORY BY MICHAEL CONNOR

Monifa is in pain but does not think anything is broken. She is more shaken up, winded and a little scared. Picking wild greens and collecting small grubs, close to the edge she has stepped on the dried biscuity earth and it has given way. When she was younger and her sight was clearer, she would not have trod on that spot or had she, she would have skipped free with a giggle.

Those days are as fresh a memory as building the fire before she set out to forage; before she had mothered Olabode twenty five years ago. He is coming back today. Back on the ferry, across the water, and then by cart over the stoney track from the village at the foot of the valley. For all she knows he might already be there, sharing a drink with people he has not seen for the years he has been away.

The greens have blown well out of reach, and the grubs scattered. She sighs and sees the dust puff around her nose and lips as she does so. Her cheek is grazed and she has not the strength to lift her head, let alone her body. What will her boy think of her when she greets him with blood dried on her face masking the smile, the joy of seeing him again.

Ten minutes pass. She makes the effort. Taking hold of a clump of grasses and then a length of exposed root, Monifa pushes down with her foot to see if the narrow ledge she has stopped on will hold her full weight if she were to stand. It seems to. Nervously, she starts to bring herself upright. It holds. She realises she has slipped further, deeper, and the climb back is only going to be achieved with some difficulty.

First she is pleased, each move takes her nearer the top. There have been no setbacks although she can see she still has a good height to cover. She rests and sees the sun has moved further than she would have imagined. The worry churns in her belly. Realising, as the wind has picked up, the liquor in the big iron pot perched over the fire will be boiling its guts out. Fanned flames will boil it dry, and then the meat will stick to the bottom, quickly turning into a hard charred log. That piece of meat had been so hard to come by. She made sacrifices. Worked hard to collect valuables she could barter in the village, from the moment she received the news of Olabode's visit. Now it will be ruined if she can't get back shortly and douse the heat.

Monifa eats meat rarely. Paki, her husband, Olabode's father, would shoot twice a week. And in those days, small animals and birds would always be hanging in the cooking corner, at the far end of the single stone room that was their family home. Since his death, a year after their son had struck out on his own to conquer the world, little meat went into the pot. Monifa had tried with the gun, but shooting hurt her shoulder and her aim was so off, the results burnt up more energy than was provided. Birds' eggs and grubs form most of the protein in her diet.

She knows if she is to rescue the meal specially prepared, she must climb faster. But the wind is gusting, mischievously pulling and pushing at her as she seeks a new handhold, stoking her fear that the fire will be roaring. The pot burning dry.

If it burns she will have nothing to place before her wonderful boy, and after such a long journey. What kind of mother will he think she has become. Even the grubs she was intending to cook for breakfast were lost. At this time of year, the birds swooping were formidable and skilled collectors of nourishment. She and the birds had crossed on many occasions.

Vicious beaks, savage squawking and the wild flapping punctuated the assault she underwent to steal the eggs. The climb to a nest lodged below her reach had been every bit as arduous as that of her present predicament. First scaling down, and then scrambling back up, protecting her fragile treasure while under sustained attack. But it was those eggs, those specific eggs, the dealer in the village demanded for the payment of good money. The kind of money the butcher demanded for such a large cut of imported red meat, that now graced her pot. The wonderfully tender meat she would proudly place on the table, if she could just get back to the fire before it turned to cinder rock.

Then even the beaks and talons will find it impossible to master.

The sun seems to be dropping a rung at a time. On other afternoons she would sit in front of her house and watch the flaming orange globe sink gently below the mountain that formed the ridge on the other side of the valley. She would sip a warm infusion, watch the sky turn red and listen to messages being whistled across and along the length of the rift, as those who lived and scratched an existence communicated their view on the day or their hopes for tomorrow.

Monifa wonders if she should whistle a call for assistance. But what was the point. If she took her time she is confident she can make the ascent long before help could arrive from her nearest neighbour. And anyway she is parched, she will need a big guzzle of liquid before she can even consider going down that route.

Sitting, thinking, she tells herself it is a waste of time. And time is the one thing she knows is in short supply. Turning to face inwards again from the sitting position she has taken up, resting her hind quarters on a protruding rock, she stretches up, pulls, reaches higher with the other hand, pulls again, then rubs her ankle along the face until her foot locates another resting place. Repeating this movement she manoeuvres her way up and along, up and along. Grasping, pulling, stretching.

Now the sun is starting to sit directly on the mountain top. Shadows are already creeping across the crags and foliage far below. Her eyes search along the valley for a cart heading in her direction. Olabode will have some sort of light mounted. It is a long time since he has made the trip, and the road changes with each rainy season. There is no light. Monifa is wondering if maybe he has already arrived. But she knows this can't be the case. Finding the house deserted and fire under the pot Olabode would have whistled out his presence.

Paki had warned his son before he left. It was well known that as soon as young men travelled away it did not take long for their minds to fill with other things, and the art of the whistling language was soon forgotten. This would not be the case with him Olabode assured his father; certain he was that he would pass on his knowledge to his own children.

She thinks now she remembered Paki saying the same to his father when he had first left and she had thought she would never see the boy she watched every day, ever again. But he had returned and she had persuaded him to stay. Although she is not sure. Maybe this is purely her imagination.

Porridge is all there is in the kitchen. Even the poorest of the villagers did not serve porridge without relish. Everything she had was put into the pot. The thick relish simmering over the flames, the juices from the meat as it became tender providing flavour and thickening. Then it will all be placed on the table, for them to share. Olabode will carve the meat into small cubes, and with fingers they will mould the bland balls of porridge and dip them into the relish. A meal fit to place before the richest.

The sun is now cut in half, the valley almost completely dark. She can see two lights, maybe three, but it is impossible to tell if any are Olabode or truly if any are climbing on the higher track. One must be, she decides.

She tries to return her attention to the matter in hand. She doesn't want to be still climbing in the dark. She scrabbles on. As she does so, she notices that with the failing daylight the wind has also dropped. She considers the possibility that the heat has also come out of the fire. She knows it makes little difference, she has been away from the kitchen far too long. But still she places one hand over the other fast and faster.

The root on which her weight is held shakes loose and falls away. Now though, her fingers are gripping over the top, her hands pull into bunches, her elbows dig in at the same moment her feet swing free. Straining hard, bending her legs, her frail body is there, crouching, kneeling, standing, she is there.

Proud, she looks down over the edge and seeing how far she has come tells herself she still has fire in her belly for the old woman she has become.

Monifa knows she has the clean clothes she laid out first thing. There will be no hot water to wash away the dirt, but her skin is hot and the cold of water drawn fresh from the barrel she will welcome.

A hundred yards off she can see no smoke, no glow of embers in the distance. She guesses the wind has whipped up the flames into a scorching heat, boiled everything dry before dying.

If she can smell the burnt food as she approaches she thinks she will cry. But the wind, now a light breeze, is wafting off across the plateau in the opposite direction.

The black pot stands alone. Suspended high over the pyramid of sticks and logs. Monifa approaches, creeping quietly. Tip-toeing close. Not sure in the dark what it is she is seeing. No heat is coming off the lid.

She lengthens her arm and touches the knob gently so as not to burn her hand. Can it be true she asks herself as her fingers grasp the cold iron. Slowly she lifts the lid. In the pale light, she imagines she can see the liquid, still clear, as clear as when she poured it in. The meat, a cushion of deep red flesh as it had been cut by the butcher's blade. And a bed of vegetables, not charred, but glistening fresh and crisp.

Monifa slams the lid closed, jumps back, stamps her feet and shouts out loud to herself and anyone or anything within hearing, that she was a stupid old woman. She has forgotten to light the fire and now there is no time to cook the food before her son arrives and he will have no supper.

Everywhere is silent. Monifa goes inside, removes her dirty clothes and using a wet towel cleans her body all the time cursing herself for being so stupid. She sits on her bed naked, and decides that at least she can chop the vegetables, get the fire started and prepare the meatless relish she usually eats. The meat will have to wait until tomorrow.

Inside the whistle is not clear, and she knows her hearing is less than it once was. The stone walls, built to keep out the heat and withhold the warmth, also dull the sounds. She pulls on her clothes and swallows a cup of water. She will whistle back a welcome to her son as he comes up the valley.

Outside she waits for the shrill sharp tones to be repeated. She gives a low whistle out into the darkness.

I am listening.

Moments later it comes again

Bad weather. Ferry delayed till tomorrow.

THE MUSHROOM EFFECT GLOSSARY

A

Abbacchio: Italian – baby lamb

Abitante del villaggio: Italian – Villager, possibly used to indicate important villager

Aboyer: French culinary term – barker – person calling food order at pass to the kitchen chefs.

Absolut: Trade name of premium vodka

Amuse Bouche : French culinary term – small savoury item served before meal to excite the mouth / appetite

Andro: Lesbian slang – Andro/Androgynous: A "unisex" lesbian (not butch or femme).

Anguilla: Italian – Eel

Arrosto: Italian cookery term – roast

Aspic: A savoury jelly often used to hold other ingredients.

B

Bain marie: French culinary term – Hot water bath for cooking slowly.

Basilicata Canestrato: Italian sheep and goats milk cheese.

Bene: Italian – Good

Benzos: Class of psychoactive drugs is mixture of a benzene and diazepine. A tranquiliser.

Beta Blockers: Drug used to counteract high blood pressure, anxiety, and tremors.

Beurre noir: French – black butter – being butter lightly burnt

Blow job: Slang – Fellatio – oral sex act performed on a man

Bog: UK slang – toilet

Bollock: Slang – testicle

Bon vivant : French phrase – a person who enjoys the good life, possibly overindulges particularly in food and wine.

Bound: 1996 American neo-noir crime thriller feature, directorial debut Lana and Lilly Wachowski. Jennifer Tilly stars.

Brasato: Italian cookery term – braised

Breeder: Lesbian slang mainly US – Heterosexual

British Lop Pig: West County white breed which grows easily and finishes as a well-muscled, lean as pork or bacon. Ideal for small scale quality farming.

Budino: Italian – pudding / desert

Burner: Mobile 'pay as you go' phone not registered to user. Can be thrown away i.e. burned

Buttinskies: US slang for person who *buts-in*, nosy person, troublesome

C

Calamaro: Italian – squid

Campylobacter: Bacteria – a common cause of food poisoning. Infection of the gut, leading to diarrhoea and vomiting. Mostly found in chicken.

Caterwauling: to cry like a cat / bawl

Casa: Italian – home

Cazzo: Italian slang – vulgar used as 'shit' would be in English

Cena: Italian – dinner

Cerimonia: Italian – ceremony

Champignon : French term – Mushroom

Chicken out: Slang – deciding at last minute not to do something because of being afraid.

Chinwag: UK slang – a chat – conversation usually pleasant.

Cognoscente: Expert / connoisseur – Italian origin but also used in English

Cold turkey: Slang – Detox – stopping drug / alcohol addiction immediately, rather than reducing consumption gradually over a period of time.

Confit: French culinary term – cooking food in fat, oil or a water syrup at a low temperature under 85c. Traditionally rubbed in salt and cooked in own fat.

Coniglio: Italian – rabbit

Costruttore artigianale: Italian – crafts manufacturer/artisan tradesman

Coulis: French culinary term widely used UK – a thick sauce created from fruit or vegetables.

Cornuto: Italian slang – cuckold, literally 'horned' – refers to a person whose spouse is cheating.

Crudo: Italian – raw

Cucina povera: Italian phrase meaning peasant cookery / rustic

Culo: Italian slang - Arse (UK) Ass (US)

D

Damascus blade: made from multiple types of steel and iron slices welded together to create a billet. Not from Damascus – a style of blacksmithing. Highly valued chefs knives are made in this style.

De rigueur : French – Current fashion

Dio: Italian – God

E

Earworm: Involuntary Musical Imagery (INMI) – a catchy piece of music continually repeats in the mind after it has stopped playing.
Epicurean: After the Greek Epicurus. A lover of fine food and wine.

F

Farmacia: Italian – pharmacy / chemist / drug store (US)

Femme: Lesbian slang – Feminine lesbian.

Ficus carica: Latin – fig tree

Fig: Italian slang – vagina – (many other uses / fruit in plural – fichi)

Flambed: French culinary term – flamed in a pan, usually with the use of a spirit.

Focaccia: Flat baked Italian bread similar texture to pizza doughs. It may be topped with herbs, salt and oil.

Formaggio: Italian – cheese

Friture: French culinary term – fryer / frying

Frullato: Italian culinary term – whipped

Fugu: Japanese name of pufferfish. Famous for being deadly, if it's not prepared correctly.

G

Garden of England: Name given to county of Kent in south east England

Giochi preferito: Italian – favourite game

Granchio: Italian – crab

Grand Cru: French term – wine of the most superior quality also used unofficially for high grade food items.

Guardie e Lardi: Italian – Italian children's game – Cops and Robbers

H

I

Imbottito: Italian culinary term – stuffed

Incanestrato: Sicilian cheese of goat and cow's milk. Aged Incanestrato commonly known as Pecorino Siciliano

Interrogatorio: Italian – interrogation

ISO :The International Organisation for Standardization

J

Jake: Slang – all fine/OK/Alright

John: Slang – prostitute's customer

Jupiter Ascending: 2015 space opera film written, produced and directed by The Wachowskis. Starring Mila Kunis.

K

Kip: Slang – sleep

L

Lam: (on the) US slang – on the run, fugitive, outsider

Lauro: Italian – bay leaf (herb)

Liqueur de Pamplemousse Rosé: French liqueur made using pink grapefruit

Little Boy and Fat Man: Name given to each of the two nuclear bombs dropped on Japan in World War 2

Loo: Slang – toilet

Loony bin: Mental hospital

M

Marinato: Italian – Marinate / pickle

Media Cottura: medium cooked

Mille feuille : French name of a cream or custard slice made using multi-leaf crispy puff pastry.

Mis en plus: French cookery term for food preparation prior to service.

Misto: Italian – mixed

Modus operandi: Method of doing something, usually habitual.

Morto: Italian – dead

Mumpish: Casual English – sullen

N

Necking (a drink): Slang – getting it (the liquid) down your neck or drinking from the neck of the bottle

Nonna: Italian – grandmother

Normandy Beurre de Baratte: Hand-moulded high quality butter from the Isigny region of Normandy, France

O

Oca bumps: Italian – goose bumps

Oh Wonder: London alt-pop band, with Josephine Vander Gucht and Anthony West

Onion skins: Refers a thin, light-weight, strong, often translucent paper. Not made from onions

Osso buco: Italian – Braised veal shank with vegetables, white wine broth

OTT: Over The Top, 'too much'.

P

Parisienne spoon: French culinary term – used to scoop out ball from food in preparation i.e. raw potato.

Parolacce: Italian – Bad language

Petto: Italian –breast
Poissonnier: French culinary term – Head of fish corner

Poppa: Lesbian slang – A young lesbian probably underage

Posso avere ancora un po' di vino?: Italian – Can I have some more wine?

Pufferfish: See Fugu

Puking: Slang – vomiting
Pranzo: Italian - lunch

Primi dish: Italian culinary term – usually refers to a starter / first course on the menu – often pasta served after the antipasti

Pruneaux dans une chemise: French – Prunes in a shirt - prunes wrapped in bacon

Q

R

Raviolo: Single pasta filled pouch, usually larger than the multiple ravioli (plural) served.

Rolling Rock: Trade name US lager

S

Salamander: French culinary term for a grill with overhead electricity or gas infrared heating elements.
Salsiccia:Italian - sausage

Salsa verde: Italian green sauce made with herbs

Saucier (sauté chef): French culinary term - Chef responsible for all sautéed items and sauces. Considered the most demanding, responsible, and glamorous corner of the kitchen.

Sauté: French culinary term - fry quickly in a little oil / butter

Scandi : Short for Scandinavian.

Scoreggia: Italian - flatulence

Scouse: UK Slang term for person from Liverpool

Scrogging: Stealing fruit from fields / orchards

Scuola di catechismo: Italian - Sunday school

Secondi : Italian culinary term - usually refers to main course on menu normally meat.

Servizio: Italian - service

Shit-face: Incredibly drunk, also obnoxious person.

Sommelier(s): French term - Wine waiter(s) with expert knowledge of wines and the pairing of wines with food.

Sourdough: Bread made from a fermented dough. Good flavour and ideal for sandwiches, toast and bruschetta.

Stracciato: Italian cookery term - scrambled

Strega comanda color: Italian children's game - witch calls the colour

Stud: Lesbian slang - a dominant lesbian, usually butch.

Stupido: Italian - stupid

Sucs: French cookery term for deglazing, is a technique for removing browned food residue from a roasting pan

T

Tagine: A Maghrebi (N African) dish named after the conical earthenware pot in which it is cooked.

Terrazza: Italian - terrace

Thimithi: A festival where people wall over hot coals

Timo: Italian - thyme   (herb)

Top (on): Lesbian slang - dominant position / person during sex

U

V

Vastedda della Valle del Belice: Sheep's milk cheese from Sicily

Vino bianco: Italian - white wine

Virgin Mary: Non alcoholic cocktail based on Bloody Mary cocktail

W

Wachowskis's Sense8: Lana & Lilly Wachowskis are both trans women film directors of acclaimed Sense8 scifi drama.

Wank: Slang - masturbate

Wallyo: Italian slang - of Italian origin, not born in Italy

White horses: Expression indicating waves in the sea are breaking with white surf tips.

X

Y

Z

Zebrune banana shallots: Technically an onion bulb, elongated, brown-skinned with a pinkish tinge, easy to chop. Delicious to eat.

Zimino: Italian - fish stew

Zuppa di Pesce: Italian - fish soup

ABOUT THE AUTHOR

Michael Connor is a freelance writer specialising in food, travel and crime issues. He is hotel-school trained and has spent lengthy periods in Africa (including Zimbabwe, Zambia and Sierra Leone), China, Greece and the former Republic of Yugoslavia, the Caribbean and the UK.

He has researched and written a full-page weekly feature for the *Caterer and Hotelkeeper* magazine over a six-year period, plus a variety of pieces for *Now* magazine, *GQ*, *Adrenalin*, *FT*, the *Guardian*, the *Mirror* and the *News of the World*.

Michael Connor is a member of English PEN, which promotes free speech, human rights and greater understanding through literature.

www.michael-connor.co.uk

OTHER PUBLICATIONS
FROM OUEN PRESS

Crime thrillers...

IMAGINE GHOSTS TELLING TALES IN FRONT OF SMOKY MIRRORS *by S.L.Masunda* – is a fictional memoir exploring a writer's quest for literary recognition. The atrocities he commits in the name of ambition become increasingly gruesome, but we are drawn back in time to reveal pivotal moments in the writer's life that challenge the reader to seek out redemption for our hero turned killer.

MAY ALL YOUR NAMES BE FORGOTTEN *by Michael Connor* – a fast moving crime thriller set in south London, containing as many pointers for budding telesales staff, prepared to break the rules, as it does for the ordinary citizen seeking to avoid being hustled.

Other rites of passage...

THE CLEANSING *by Michael Connor* – weaves a powerful plot, full of vivid encounters and fascinating characters. It depicts the harsh reality that still faces many, particularly the women, in Africa today.

Short story collection...

TASTING NOTES *including Ouen Press Short Story Competition Winners 2017* – a complex and diverse menu of science fiction, art, humour, the spying game, magical realism, celebrity cooking and much more, expertly crafted to tantalise and entertain.

All books available from good bookshops,
and Amazon in paperback & ebook.

www.ouenpress.com